Elizabeth entered the courtroom. With relief, she sank into a seat next to her father at a long, narrow table in front.

Mr. Wakefield approached the bench, as did the district attorney who was arguing the case against her. Elizabeth watched the judge and the two lawyers converse in low tones. *It's like a made-for-TV* movie, she thought, feeling dazed and helpless. *It's a movie and I've been assigned a part, but I don't have a script. I don't know anyone's lines. I don't know what's going to happen.*

Judge Baird struck her desk with a gavel. The sound echoed ominously throughout the courtroom; Elizabeth's heart jumped. Instantly, an expectant hush fell over the audience. "Court is now in session," the judge pronounced. Elizabeth closed her eyes, mentally preparing herself. *This is it. . . .*

Bantam Books in the Sweet Valley High series
Ask your bookseller for the books you have missed

THE VERDICT

**Written by
Kate William**

**Created by
FRANCINE PASCAL**

BANTAM BOOKS
NEW YORK · TORONTO · LONDON · SYDNEY · AUCKLAND

RL 6, age 12 and up

THE VERDICT

A Bantam Book / August 1993

Sweet Valley High® *is a registered trademark of Francine Pascal*
Conceived by Francine Pascal
Produced by Daniel Weiss Associates, Inc.
33 West 17th Street
New York, NY 10011
Cover art by Joe Danisi

ISBN: 0-553-29854-2

Published simultaneously in the United States and Canada

Bantam Books are published by Bantam Books, a division of Bantam Doubleday Dell Publishing Group, Inc. Its trademark, consisting of the words "Bantam Books" and the portrayal of a rooster, is Registered in U.S. Patent and Trademark Office and in other countries. Marca Registrada. Bantam Books, 1540 Broadway, New York, New York 10036.

PRINTED IN THE UNITED STATES OF AMERICA

OPM   0 9 8 7 6 5 4 3 2 1

Chapter 1

"OK, Elizabeth. Take a deep breath and try to relax."

Elizabeth Wakefield did as she was told even though she knew it wouldn't help. Her stomach was tied in knots and every muscle in her body was tense. *How can I relax when the day after tomorrow I stand trial for manslaughter?* she wondered, her blue-green eyes wide and blank as she stared at her attorney, who also happened to be her father.

She gulped in some air and lifted her golden-blond ponytail off her neck. "That's good," Mr. Wakefield said. He gave her shoulder a quick squeeze, then resumed pacing nervously in front of the sofa. "You know what I have to do in order to

1

mount an effective defense on Tuesday," he began, keeping his voice low and soothing. "You know what *you* have to do. We need to piece together the complete story of what happened the night of the Jungle Prom."

Elizabeth nodded, the knots in her stomach tightening painfully. "I know," she whispered and took another deep, shaky breath. *I do need to remember,* she told herself. *If I don't want to be locked up in a juvenile home for months or even years, I have to remember!*

"OK, then. Let's try again. Tell me what you remember," her father urged. "Start at the beginning. Take your time."

Tell me what you remember. . . . The words echoed in Elizabeth's brain. She'd heard them so many times before; so many people had used the exact-same words! The officers at the Sweet Valley police station after the accident, her parents, her older brother, Steven, the defense attorney her family had hired and then fired when he recommended that she plead guilty to the charges brought against her. "What happened that night?" they'd asked, over and over and over until she wanted to scream. "Tell me what you remember."

"You were with Sam at the prom," Mr. Wakefield prompted his daughter.

Elizabeth bit her lip. *No, I was with Todd,* she

2

thought. But she had danced with Sam Woodruff, her twin sister's boyfriend, while Todd Wilkins, her own boyfriend, was off being crowned Prom King.

"Sam and I were dancing," Elizabeth said aloud. "I remember that. . . ."

"Good. And then you left the dance together," Mr. Wakefield continued. "Jessica and Todd both saw you go. You and Sam went to the parking lot and got into the Jeep. Do you remember that?"

Elizabeth knew it must have happened the way her father described it. She and Sam must have gotten into the Jeep, and then she must have driven out of the parking lot and down the road. But she couldn't remember actually *doing* those things; it was always at this point that her memory grew fuzzy and dim.

She shook her head. "No. I . . . I don't remember that part."

Mr. Wakefield raked a hand through his dark hair. "You've got to remember *something*, Liz," he pressed, struggling to contain his frustration. "Can you remember when you and Sam started drinking? Or what caused you to drive off the road? Was there another car involved? Think, honey. Think *hard*. You've got to help me help you"

Elizabeth squeezed her eyes shut, trying desperately to conjure up a picture of what had transpired that fateful night. In her mind's eye, she saw

3

flashing lights and blood and shattered glass and crumpled metal. She heard the wail of sirens. But only because she knew what the scene must have been like. She couldn't *remember* it, but she could *imagine* it—too clearly.

"I can't," Elizabeth whispered, curling her hands into tight fists. "I just can't."

It was the truth. The last thing Elizabeth remembered with any distinctness was dancing with Sam at the Jungle Prom. She'd danced with happy abandon because she'd decided to drop out of the running for Prom Queen, letting Jessica win the crown and the trip to Brazil that both sisters had coveted and fought over. It had definitely been their worst battle ever, but out on the dance floor Elizabeth's reasons for wanting the Prom Queen title had simply fallen away. "I don't need to compete with Jessica," she remembered saying to Sam. "I like myself just the way I am."

Her decision had just felt right. She and Jessica, while identical in looks, had very different priorities. Jessica was her happiest when at the center of attention, and Elizabeth was more of a behind-the-scenes kind of person. "I organized a great prom, but Jessica was *born* to be Prom Queen." Laughing, Sam had hugged her. He'd been a good friend to her, and she knew he'd loved Jessica dearly. And Jessica had loved him, too, so much.

But she could only recall the dancing—Elizabeth didn't even remember leaving the prom with her sister's boyfriend, let alone driving away with him. And she couldn't remember losing control of the Jeep. Had she screamed? Had Sam? Had he died instantly, or had he suffered?

Tears flooded Elizabeth's eyes. "I don't know how we got drunk, Dad, honest. I only remember the dance. I don't remember a single thing about the . . . the accident." She choked back an anguished sob. "I'm sorry. I'm just so sorry."

For a moment, her father hung his head, his jaw clenched. Elizabeth knew that he, too, was struggling with frustration and despair.

But Ned Wakefield wasn't going to give up. Lifting his eyes, he strode across the room to sit beside her. "We'll win this thing, Liz," he vowed, taking her hands in his. "If it's the last thing I do, I'll get you acquitted. I promise you."

Elizabeth nodded, but in her heart she felt hopeless. Was there really anything anyone, even her devoted father, could do for her?

Elizabeth's eyes flickered across the room as a shadow momentarily darkened the door to the hallway. She caught a brief glimpse of a slim, blond girl—her own mirror image—as Jessica passed by on her way to the staircase. Jessica didn't pause; she didn't even glance into the room.

Elizabeth wanted to run after her, but she knew it wouldn't do any good. *It's too late,* she thought, and she turned her head so her father wouldn't see the tear rolling down her cheek. *What is done cannot be undone.* She had killed her sister's boyfriend. Jessica hated her for it, and would never forgive her. As for Todd . . . Another hot tear spilled from Elizabeth's eye. She'd lost him, too.

I don't blame them for hating me. I'm poison. Evil. I killed Sam, and I've torn my family apart.

Her own life, which had once seemed so perfect, was now completely shattered. Pretty, popular, talented Elizabeth Wakefield's world in the picture-perfect town of Sweet Valley, California, had turned into a living nightmare.

Todd tapped the brakes of the black BMW, slowing as he coasted into the dimly lit parking lot by the beach. As he pulled in, Todd saw that it was nearly deserted; there was only one other car parked at the far end. He recognized the car—she'd been driving her mother's since the Jeep got wrecked.

Killing the engine, Todd climbed out of the BMW and walked with slow, purposeful strides across the parking lot. As he drew closer to the other car, the driver's side door opened and a girl in a leather jacket stepped out.

For a moment, he could almost pretend. They

looked so much alike. . . . She was five foot six and slender. The same breeze that stirred the grass on the dunes made her pale blond hair dance around her shoulders; in the moonlight, her blue-green eyes glimmered like jewels. As Todd approached, she smiled in shy welcome, a tiny dimple creasing her left cheek. *Elizabeth,* Todd thought, a hopeless longing filling his heart.

But it wasn't Elizabeth.

Todd took her hands in his and pulled her close, wrapping her in a protective embrace. "Hi, Jess," he murmured into her silky, blond hair.

Later that night, Jessica lay on her bed in the dark, staring up at the ceiling. A cool breeze rustled the leaves of the trees and stirred the curtains at the open window. Other than that the night was quiet . . . dead quiet.

She rolled over, staring now at the illuminated numerals of the clock radio on her bedside table. Two o'clock in the morning. *Will I ever fall asleep?* Jessica wondered drearily. Every night it was the same. She tossed and turned for hours, and when she finally did doze off, it was even worse than staying awake. In her sleep the nightmares came— nightmares about the Jungle Prom and the Prom Queen's crown and the crash and the funeral, about Sam and Elizabeth and Todd . . .

Sam . . .

She turned over once more, threw back her covers, and swung her legs over the side of the bed. "I might as well get up," she mumbled to herself, slipping her arms into the sleeves of her terrycloth robe. "I'm going to be a zombie at school tomorrow, anyway."

She padded out into the shadowy hallway. Elizabeth's bedroom door was closed and so was her parents'. All was dark and still.

Downstairs, however, Jessica spied a glimmer of light coming from the kitchen. She found her mother sitting at the kitchen table, a needle and thread in her hand. "Hello, Jessica," Alice Wakefield greeted her daughter.

"Can't sleep either, huh, Mom?" Jessica asked sympathetically.

"Oh, no, I'm fine," Mrs. Wakefield said, bright and casual, as if it were the most normal thing in the world to be sitting at the kitchen table in the middle of the night. She held up a dress shirt of her husband's that was missing a button. "I just wanted to take care of this mending."

Jessica raised her eyebrows. "At two A.M.?"

"There's no time like the present," Mrs. Wakefield chirped.

With a shiver, Jessica turned toward the cupboard and reached for a glass. She couldn't stand

8

to watch her mother cheerfully threading her needle, looking and acting like some kind of crazy lady.

She's not crazy, Jessica told herself firmly as she poured some orange juice. *She's just . . . upset.* But Jessica knew it was more than that. Her mother was barely holding herself together these days, and with Elizabeth's trial only a day away . . . What if it pushed her right over the edge?

Jessica glanced quickly over her shoulder at her mother, guilt piercing her heart. She knew that if she made up with Elizabeth, it would make both of her parents feel better, more optimistic. She knew how much her anger, her refusal to even speak to Elizabeth much less support and comfort her, upset them. And they didn't even know about Todd. . . . Jessica herself wondered how much her attitude toward her sister contributed to the fact that Elizabeth couldn't even get herself together enough to go to school. *If I could just make a token effort, for them. . . . Couldn't I do that?*

For a moment, Jessica seriously considered the possibility. Then her eyes narrowed and her heart grew hard. For her mother's pain, she had nothing but pity. But when she thought about Elizabeth, about what Elizabeth had done . . .

I can't forgive her, Jessica thought firmly. *She took Sam away from me. She killed him. Nothing, nothing, nothing can ever make up for that!*

She sipped her juice, spilling some of it because her hand was shaking. Elizabeth was guilty—it was that simple. She was going to be put on trial and the judge would find her guilty, and as awful as that was for their whole family, it was the only conceivable outcome . . . the only *fair* outcome. Wasn't it?

For a split second, a tiny measure of doubt flickered through Jessica's mind. Against her will, she envisioned herself at the prom. She remembered the boy from Big Mesa, Sweet Valley High's archrival school, sloshing a generous portion of alcohol into a paper cup. She remembered carrying the cup over to where Elizabeth had set her cup down, and pouring the alcohol into Elizabeth's punch. . . .

With an effort, Jessica pushed the memory from her consciousness. *It's not my fault. Elizabeth's the one who got in the Jeep with Sam even though she was too drunk to drive.* She *crashed.* She *killed him. Not me.*

"I was talking to your father before he went to bed," Mrs. Wakefield said conversationally. Jessica looked up with a start. "About Elizabeth's defense, and he thinks it would help if you—"

Jessica felt her face flush with anger. "No," she broke in before her mother could finish.

Mrs. Wakefield seemed to shrink back in her chair. "But, Jessica, if you would only—"

"I said no!" Jessica cried, her voice loud and harsh in the quiet house. "I can't and I won't help, Mom. I won't help her. And that's final!"

Slamming her glass down on the counter, Jessica bolted from the brightly lit kitchen into the dark hallway, leaving her mother behind.

The sun was just peeking over the edge of the horizon as the bus pulled off the highway into a small midwestern town. At the back of the bus, a teenaged girl sat slumped in her seat, her drowsy gray eyes turned toward the half-open window.

Main Street, U.S.A., Margo thought with a disdainful yawn as she watched the tidy green lawns and white picket fences give way to a row of neat storefronts. *What a snore. Thank God I don't have to live in a dump like this.*

No, she wasn't going to settle for some hick town in the middle of nowhere. She wasn't getting off this bus until it reached the end of the line. She was riding it all the way, all the way across the country to the pot of gold at the end of the rainbow, to paradise—to Los Angeles, and from there to Sweet Valley, California.

"Sweet Valley," Margo murmured out loud. The words tasted good in her mouth. It just had to be a beautiful town, sweet and beautiful, full of sweet and beautiful people—nothing like the dreary, dead-end places she'd lived before. *And once I get there*, I'll *be sweet and beautiful, too,* Margo thought dreamily. *I'll start my life over, and this time I'll be perfect, just like her. . . .*

She reached next to her for her shoulder bag, which she'd put on the empty seat in order to discourage anyone from sitting there. Pulling the bag onto her lap, she hugged it possessively. It held all her treasures, all she'd managed to acquire since she'd left Long Island after the fire. The antique jewelry she'd stolen from Mrs. Smith's safe, which she couldn't wait to pawn in California; a wad of cash from the old lady's purse from the bus station back in Cleveland; and the picture she'd torn from the same old lady's newspaper.

The picture . . .

Carefully, Margo removed the black-and-white newspaper photo from her wallet. The caption was torn off, as was the accompanying story. All that was left were the face and the name.

But the face and the name were enough. They were perfect—*she* was perfect. *Elizabeth Wakefield*, Margo mused. *Elizabeth Wakefield of Sweet Valley, California*. A smile played on Margo's lips, a smile identical to that of the girl in the photograph. *This is the only difference between us, Elizabeth Wakefield*, Margo thought, twining a strand of her dark hair around her finger. *Yours is blond and mine is black.* The tiny dimple in Margo's left cheek deepened. *The only difference. And soon . . .*

With a slow screech of brakes, the bus rumbled to a stop in front of a depot on the edge of town. The driver stepped out to load some luggage, then reboarded along with three new passengers. Before Margo could again cover up the seat next to her, an elderly man settled into it.

The bus lurched forward in a cloud of dust and exhaust. Margo shifted in her seat, turning her back to the old man and curling her body around her shoulder bag. Soon they were back on the highway, and as the bus picked up speed, she looked out the window at the farmland. In the warm, gentle light of dawn, the fields looked lush and green. But there were so many of them, and the land was *so* flat. *Cornfield, cornfield, cornfield,* Margo counted silently. *How ugly. How monotonous.*

"Beautiful mornin'," remarked the old man next to her.

Margo glanced at him out of the corner of her eye. He was sitting erect, his hands folded neatly on top of the cane that was propped between his bony knees, a brown paper bag resting on his lap. "Hmm," she mumbled, her tone anything but friendly.

13

"Yep, it's a good year for growin' things," the man continued, cheerfully oblivious to her scowl. "The corn is as high as an elephant's eye," he chuckled. "You from around here?" he asked Margo.

No, thank God, Margo felt like blurting out. *So, shut up and leave me alone, you dried-up old fool!*

But she caught herself before the harsh words could escape her lips. *Be careful—be very, very careful,* she counseled herself. It wouldn't do to draw attention to herself, to provoke suspicion. She had to stay in control. If she didn't, someone might take a closer look at her. Someone might retrace her steps, back to the bus station and the old woman, strangled with her own scarf; back to the lake in Ohio and little Georgie Smith's drowned body; back to the looted safe in the Smiths' home; all the way back, even, to Long Island and the fire that had started mysteriously and consumed Margo's old foster home and the body of a small girl, her little foster sister Nina. . . .

"No," Margo said out loud, her voice softer. "I'm not from around here. I'm from. . ." *Not New York. Not Ohio.* "From Pennsylvania."

"And where are you going, er . . . ?"

"Judith," said Margo. "My name is Judith Brown, and I'm going to Los Angeles to find my mother."

14

The old man's wrinkled, papery face lit up with curiosity. "To find your mother?"

He wants a story, Margo guessed, suppressing a grim smile. What would he think if she told him the truth—if she told him about her life as an abandoned child shipped from one foster home to another, about the abuse she'd suffered at the hands of older "brothers" and even foster parents—if she told him about the crimes she'd had to commit in order to break free?

He wanted to hear a story, but not that story. No one wanted to hear *that* story, least of all Margo herself. That was why she was starting a *new* life. She'd left the old life behind, taking away nothing but the survival skills her pain and deprivation had bequeathed to her.

She turned with sweet, melancholy eyes to the old man. "My mother gave me away when I was born," she explained. "I don't blame her. She was very young, and not married."

The old man clucked his tongue. "You poor thing."

"I'm not the one you should feel sorry for," Margo told him. "Think of how hard it was for *her*, a young girl from a small town, pregnant and deserted by the boy she loved, with no one to turn to, no place to go. She left me one cold winter's day— Christmas Eve, actually—on the steps of a church, bundled in a blanket. And she was never seen or heard from again."

He clucked his tongue again. "Oh, my."

Margo continued with the fiction, enjoying her story. "I was truly fortunate, however, to be raised by a very kind family, the Browns. I had everything a child could want or need. But, as much as I've loved the Browns, I never forgot that they weren't my *real* parents. I never stopped dreaming of finding my real mother someday."

"And you did? You found her?" the old man asked eagerly.

Margo nodded. "Every year at Christmas, someone made an anonymous donation to the church—the very same church where my mother left me," she said, swept away by the fantasy she was weaving. "It was never very much money—a pittance, really—but clearly it meant a lot to whoever gave it. This year, someone at the church finally decided to see if they could discover who the donor was by tracing the money order." She paused dramatically.

The old man was on the edge of his seat. "And it was her!" he exclaimed.

"It was her," Margo said softly. "You see, she hadn't forgotten me, either. Every year she sent a little something from California, where she'd gone to start a new life, hoping that somehow, in some way, it would reach me and help me."

Margo watched with satisfaction as the old man reached into his shirt pocket for a handkerchief and then dabbed at his eyes. *People are so gullible,* she thought scornfully as he blew his nose with a loud honk. *They're so easy to manipulate, to soften up, and then wrap around your finger.*

They rode in silence for a while, until the bus pulled off the highway again. A minute later, it rattled to a stop in the middle of another town that looked exactly like the last one. The old man shuffled to his feet. "This is where I get off, dear," he informed Margo. "I wish I could get you over to my sister's. She'd cook you up a nice hot breakfast—put some meat on your bones. You have such a long way to go, and all by yourself. . . ."

"I'll be all right," Margo assured him, allowing her voice to tremble just a tiny bit.

"Well . . . here." The old man fumbled in his pocket for his wallet. Pulling out a bill, he pressed it into Margo's hand.

"Oh, no," she demurred, dropping her eyes shyly. "Really, I can't—"

"I insist." He folded her fingers around the bill, squeezing her hand. "And so you don't go hungry while you're on the road—" He pushed the brown paper bag toward her. "—one of my sister's sandwiches. It'll tide you over till suppertime."

"Thank you," Margo said, acting grateful and embarrassed. "Thank you very much, sir."

The old man started down the aisle, his cane tapping. "Good luck to you, dear," he called back to her.

Margo lifted her hand in a wave. The old man stepped down to the sidewalk and the bus roared off.

Margo watched the man's figure grow smaller and smaller, until he was just a tiny doll, and then a speck, and then nothing. Unclenching her fist, she looked at the bill he'd given her. *Five bucks—big deal*, she thought. Still, cash was cash. She'd need every penny she could get.

Margo tucked the money into her bag, then opened the old man's paper sack. Inside was a fat turkey sandwich in plastic wrap. Lifting the sandwich to her nose, she gave it a disdainful sniff and tossed it out the open window.

Chapter 2

"I still can't believe it," Caroline Pearce said, her green eyes somber. "I can't believe this is happening here in Sweet Valley, and to the Wakefields of all people! I keep thinking one of these days we'll all wake up and find out we've been having some kind of collective nightmare."

The faces of her friends, gathered in the hall of Sweet Valley High on Monday morning before homeroom, were equally solemn. "It's a nightmare, all right, but we're wide awake and living through it," Amy Sutton, one of Jessica's two best friends, remarked grimly, shaking her head at the open newspaper in front of her.

Just then Lila Fowler, Jessica's other best

friend, arrived and pushed forward to get a look at the front-page headline of that day's *Sweet Valley News*. "'Wakefield Manslaughter Trial Starts Tomorrow,'" she read out loud. Lila shivered. "Manslaughter trial—they make it sound like she's a serial killer or something!"

"Poor Elizabeth," Caroline murmured. She pointed to the photograph underneath the headline. "She looks awful. How will she ever have the strength to testify?"

Lila studied the picture of her best friend's twin sister leaving the courtroom after the arraignment a few days earlier. Elizabeth's eyes were deeply shadowed and her once sun-streaked blond hair hung limply around a thin, unsmiling face that even in the grainy image looked as pale as milk. "Her clothes are practically falling off her," Lila observed. "I bet she's lost five or ten pounds since . . ."

Lila's voice trailed off. *Since the night everything changed forever,* she thought to herself. She wondered if any of them, if anybody at Sweet Valley High, would ever forget that night. She knew she never would.

And I thought I'd been having a bad night, Lila reflected, wryly. She was thinking about Nathan Pritchard, a counselor at the high school who'd chaperoned the Jungle Prom. Nathan had worked with Lila at Project Youth, helping her sort through her feelings after she was nearly raped by her classmate John Pfeifer. At the prom, when the brawl broke out between Sweet Valley and Big Mesa students, Nathan had tried to get Lila out of the fray, to safety. Alone with Nathan, all her fear and confusion about her near rape resurfaced and she'd freaked out. When the police arrived, Lila had accused Nathan of trying to attack her.

It was bad, all right, Lila mused, the voices of her friends fading in and out as they discussed the tragedy, *but in some ways it was incredibly good.* She hit emotional rock bottom that night, so from then on, there was no place to go but up. With Nathan's help, she'd confronted her problems and realized they went way beyond the incident with John Pfeifer. *And that's when Daddy called Grace in France and she came to be with me. After all these years, I finally have a mother.*

Yes, Lila decided silently, as she continued to stare at the newspaper picture of Elizabeth, *I got lucky.* For Liz and Jessica and their family, and for Sam Woodruff's parents, there was no silver lining—only tragedy.

Caroline reached into her purse for a piece of gum. "I feel so sorry for *all* of them," she said, unwrapping it. "For Jessica, losing Sam, and for Elizabeth having to go on trial. As if just knowing she was behind the wheel that night isn't punishment enough!" She shook her head.

Rosa Jameson, who had been keeping quiet until now, spoke up timidly. "Maybe the trial won't turn out so badly. Once they hear Elizabeth's side of the story—once they see for themselves that she's really a decent, responsible person . . ."

"Don't be naive, Rosa," Lila advised. "My dad says the prosecuting attorney is a real terror. He's going to eat Elizabeth for lunch."

"They can't hear Elizabeth's side of the story because she doesn't *know* her side of the story," Amy explained with exasperation. "The Jeep crashed, Sam was killed, and they were both drunk at the time. Those are the facts."

"Their being drunk—that's the part I don't understand," interjected Rosa. "I can't imagine Elizabeth ever *touching* alcohol."

"Sure, it's totally out of character," Caroline agreed. "But blood tests don't lie. She was wasted."

Rosa shook her head. "I still don't understand it. Who would have brought alcohol to the dance, and what on earth would have made her—"

At that moment, Lila spotted Jessica walking toward them. She motioned rapidly to Caroline, who quickly stuffed the newspaper back into her pack. "Hi, Jessica," Lila said brightly.

Jessica's eyes flickered over her friends' faces. "You don't have to pretend you weren't just talking about the trial," she informed them dryly. "Everybody else is—why shouldn't you?"

Caroline patted Jessica's arm. "We were only saying that we wish there was something we could do. We just want you to know we're here for you, Jess."

Jessica's lips twisted. "For me? Hey, I'm fine. I'm not the one you should worry about. *I'm* not on trial for murder."

Brushing past them, she continued on down the hall, her shoulders back and her head held high. The group of girls stared after her. "Talk about denial," murmured Amy.

Lila knew Amy liked to bandy about the psychology terms she'd learned since she'd started operating the teen hotline at Project Youth. But Lila had to agree. Jessica was suffering from a serious case of denial.

Bruce Patman elbowed his way down Sweet Valley High's crowded main hallway, heading for his locker. All around him there was a steady buzz of voices; at the same time, the atmosphere was somehow solemn.

Everyone's discussing Elizabeth's trial, Bruce guessed, a grim smile curving his lips. *Maybe we should take bets on the verdict—guilty or innocent?*

It was weird, Bruce thought. Just about the

time the accident occurred that had cost Sam his life, Bruce's own life was being saved.

And I was falling in love, Bruce thought with bitter irony. *What a fateful night.*

He frowned as he reached his locker, thinking back. His memories of that night were burned indelibly onto his brain. He knew he'd never forget them, no matter how much he wanted to—now that it was over between him and Pamela.

From the start, Bruce had known there'd be trouble at the prom. For weeks, Sweet Valley's rivalry with Big Mesa High had been growing more and more intense. The dance was open to other schools, and there had been a rumor going around that a bunch of Big Mesa kids were going to show up. Everyone knew a clash was inevitable.

Soon after Jessica was crowned Prom Queen, gangs of kids from the feuding schools poured out of the gym onto the football field. The brawl had been a wild one, and Bruce had given as good as he got . . . until the moment he was struck down from behind by a boy with a baseball bat.

Another blow might have killed him. . . . But then *she* had appeared. In his mind's eye, Bruce once again saw Pamela's beautiful, distressed face, heard her gentle voice pleading for mercy on his behalf. *Why?* he wondered. *Why had she bothered?*

She'd disappeared into the night without a

trace, but Bruce had tracked her down, convinced that she was the girl of his dreams, the one he'd been longing for ever since he'd lost Regina. And at first, she was everything he'd imagined. For the first time since Regina died, Bruce had felt he'd found someone he could truly care for. *Little did I know,* he thought as he dialed his locker combination with quick, impatient jerks of his wrist, *that my angel of mercy would turn out to be anything but innocent!*

His jaw clenched with undiminished anger as he recalled the Sunday morning when he drove over to Pamela's house to surprise her with an armful of roses. He'd surprised her, all right . . . stepping out of the car of some guy she'd obviously been with all night. Bruce had never been so humiliated; he'd never felt like such a complete and utter fool.

Grabbing the books he needed for his first class, Bruce slammed his locker shut and turned to plunge back into the stream of students. Suddenly—as if his thoughts had conjured up a living image—he found himself staring straight at Pamela Robertson.

Bruce's face flooded with heat. *Is it my imagination?* he wondered, blinking. *Am I going nuts?* No, Pamela was real and walking right toward him, clutching a stack of books and looking like any other student in the hallway . . . or rather, any other *new* student.

Clearly, she didn't know where she was going. She glanced at the lockers as she passed, reading the numbers. When she spotted Bruce, she stopped in her tracks, her bright blue eyes widening. Starting forward again, she bumped into somebody walking in the opposite direction and her books went flying.

In the few seconds it took Pamela to pick up her books, Bruce recovered his composure. This was *his* school, after all. She was the one off balance.

Pamela straightened up, flipping back her dark, tumbled hair. Seeking Bruce with her eyes, she gave him a tentative half-smile, the kind that was ready to blossom into a full smile if it met any encouragement.

It didn't. Bruce stepped toward her, but only because he had to in order to get to his homeroom. A look of disgust on his face, he brushed past Pamela without a word.

What's she doing here, anyway? he wondered as he sauntered down the hall, hoping everyone could see that Pamela Robertson meant absolutely nothing to him. *Has she slept with all the guys in Big Mesa? Did she switch schools so she could make some new conquests?*

One thing Bruce knew for sure. Pamela's reputation had preceded her to Sweet Valley High. He hadn't been the first to learn of her exploits—not by a long shot. And he had a hunch that by the end of the day—maybe even by lunchtime—Pamela was going to wish she'd stayed in Big Mesa where she belonged.

Eighty-five, eighty-six, eighty-seven—here it is. With a sigh of relief, Pamela stopped in front of her new locker at Sweet Valley High. Bending her head, she read the combination printed on the small piece of paper in her hand, glad for a chance to hide her face, which was still beet red from her encounter with Bruce.

He didn't seem too thrilled to see me, Pamela thought wryly. If only she could turn back the clock, go back in time to that Sunday morning he'd stopped by her house. . . . *But he didn't just* see *something, he* heard *the gossip, too. So I have two strikes against me, two resounding strikes. . . .*

As she opened the locker, Pamela made a conscious effort to straighten her shoulders and lift her chin. She couldn't let herself forget why she was there. It wasn't just for Bruce, although of course she was hoping he'd give her a chance to win back his respect and affection. *I'm doing this for me,* Pamela reminded herself, *I need a new start.*

She didn't want to pretend to anybody that she

was a pure and spotless angel, Pamela mused as she placed all but one of her new spiral notebooks and folders in the locker. All she wanted was a chance to change, to leave her past behind and move forward with her life. Pamela closed her locker and prepared once again to negotiate the unfamiliar corridor filled with unfamiliar faces.

Pamela paused in front of the door to her new homeroom, her heart pounding like a jackhammer. A hopeful smile touched her lips. Taking a deep breath, she stepped through the door.

Mr. Harrison, the homeroom teacher, hadn't arrived yet, but the classroom was already full, with all but a few seats in the far corner taken. As Pamela made her way toward one of the unoccupied desks, she couldn't help noticing that the hum of voices stopped abruptly. There was a moment of silence so complete it was almost loud, and then the voices started up again. But lower this time . . . whispers.

They're probably just talking about the trial, Pamela thought, feeling the color rise in her face. But along with the whispers came pointed, curious glances. Pamela had been the object of gossip too often not to know what those glances meant.

She fought the urge to turn on her heel and bolt back out into the hallway, to run as fast as her high-heeled sandals would take her out to the parking lot and all the way home to Big Mesa.

Instead, she forced herself to continue to the back of the room. She took her seat, her head still held high.

I'm going to do this, she told herself, folding her hands on top of the desk and staring straight ahead of her at the blackboard. *I'm going to stick it out, and I'm going to succeed.*

After all, there were lots of people out there who were up against much harder problems than she was, people right in this very school. Pamela thought about the poor Wakefield twins. Everyone in Big Mesa—everyone in the entire *county*—knew about what happened the night of Sweet Valley High's prom. For Pamela, it was the night she first set eyes on Bruce Patman. The boy Pamela knew she'd love forever . . . even if he never said another word to her.

Chapter 3

I wish I had an excuse to stay home from school like Liz, Jessica thought as she marched through the cafeteria, shifting her lunch tray from one hand to the other to keep from being jostled. Ordinarily, she liked being the center of attention. If kids at school ogled and admired her, it was just a reflection of the fact that she was the most popular girl at Sweet Valley High, the girl every guy wanted to date and every girl wanted to be. Today, though, Jessica could sense that the looks coming her way were of a different nature altogether. They were curious, prying, pitying. *Everyone wants to know what it feels like to have your sister on trial for accidentally killing your boyfriend.* Jessica smiled grimly as she kicked someone's backpack out of the way. *That's why people read those tacky tabloid magazines, right?*

She reached the table by the window that she'd been aiming for. Todd was sitting there, along with Bill Chase, DeeDee Gordon, Winston Egbert, and Ken Matthews. "Hi, everybody," Jessica said, slamming her tray down in between Bill and Todd.

Todd slid his chair over a few inches to make room for her. Jessica saw Bill and his girlfriend, DeeDee, exchange a glance. *They're not used to seeing me with Todd,* Jessica guessed, dropping into her chair and allowing her arm to brush Todd's in a familiar, possessive manner as she did so. *Well, take a good look, folks. Elizabeth is out of the picture—this is the way it's going to be from now on.*

"So . . ." mumbled Ken. He looked at Winston, who shrugged his shoulders. "Well, uh, like I was saying . . ."

Jessica heaved a loud, irritated sigh. "I swear, everybody must think I'm an idiot or something! I know what you were talking about before I got here, guys, and I promise you, I don't need to be protected from the topic." She laughed harshly. "I mean, I know a lot more about it than anyone else does, after all. Go ahead, pump me for information!"

Todd shifted in his chair. "We weren't talking

about anything in particular, Jessica," he said, not meeting her eyes. "We weren't talking about . . . *that*."

"You're a crummy liar, Todd," Jessica teased, giving his arm a playful squeeze. "So don't even try. What if you *were* talking about the trial? Why would I mind?"

DeeDee rested her elbows on the table and fixed sympathetic brown eyes on Jessica. "We don't want to keep reminding you of something that we know must be very painful for you," she said gently.

"Painful?" Jessica ripped the plastic wrap off of her egg-salad sandwich. "I hate to disappoint you, DeeDee, but the trial is *not* a painful subject for me." She lifted her shoulders. "Why on earth should I get upset at the idea of justice being served?"

"Justice?" Bill blurted out. "That's not the point. Liz is—"

"My sister," Jessica interrupted. "I know. Now *there's* a painful reminder."

An awkward silence fell over the table. Jessica munched on her sandwich, ignoring her friends' discomfort and the tense, uncertain glances flying among them. After a moment, Winston cleared his throat. "Well, I guess I'll be on my way. I told Maria I'd meet her. . . ."

"That's right—I have to catch up with Terri," said Ken, pushing back his chair.

33

Jessica looked expectantly at Bill and DeeDee, her expression clearly saying, "What are *your* excuses?"

"Umm . . ." DeeDee glanced at Bill. "Bill has to . . ."

"Go get some stuff together for the drama club meeting this afternoon," Bill supplied. Quickly wrapping up the remains of their lunches, they both rose to their feet. "See ya, Jess. Later, Wilkins."

Jessica watched the four hurry off. "Sorry I chased everybody off," she mumbled, suddenly feeling guilty, and anxious that Todd might desert her, too. "Well, aren't you going to follow their example?"

Todd pulled a Ziploc bag of oatmeal-raisin cookies from his lunch sack. "Naw," he said with a casual shrug. "I'm still working on my lunch." Jessica turned forlorn eyes on him. "Uh, I meant . . . I'd rather hang out with you," he added quickly.

Satisfied with this answer, she polished off her sandwich and started peeling an orange. "You know, the way everyone's acting," she remarked after a while, "you'd think they felt *sorry* for Elizabeth, like she didn't even *do* anything—like she's the victim instead of the criminal."

"She's not a criminal," Todd snapped.

Jessica stared at him. "You're not coming to her *defense*, are you?"

Todd looked down at his right hand, which had tightened into a fist, crumbling the cookie he held. "I . . . no, I just—"

"Because she wouldn't appreciate it, Todd—take my word for it." Jessica's voice grew cool. "And I don't appreciate it, either. It makes me feel like, like—" Suddenly her eyes brimmed with tears. "Like you don't care about what *I'm* going through." A sob caught in her throat and she ducked her chin, hiding behind a curtain of hair so the kids at nearby tables couldn't see her crying. "I thought—I thought you were on *my* side now."

Todd put a hand on Jessica's arm. "Of course I'm on your side," he said quietly. "But that doesn't have to mean . . ."

He didn't finish the sentence, but it was easy to guess what he'd been planning to say. "Yes, it does," Jessica said, her voice quavering with intensity. "You can't have it both ways, Todd. You can't be on her side and also on mine. You have to choose, and you *did* choose," she reminded him. She placed her hand on top of his and smiled up at him, her eyes still sparkling with tears. "Right?"

Todd hesitated for a long moment. Then his lips curved in a crooked smile. "Right," he confirmed.

Steven Wakefield surveyed the two-bedroom apartment with satisfaction. "We've really got this place looking great," he said to Billie Winkler, his new roommate. "We're ready for *Home and Garden* magazine," Billie agreed with a mischievous smile. "Their special feature on 'Coed Cohabitation off Campus; or, the Battle of the Sexes Comes to a Bathroom Near You.'"

Steven laughed, his brown eyes crinkling. "I think we've handled the culture clash pretty well so far."

Billie leaned her arms on the counter separating the little kitchen from the dining nook that was part of a larger living area. "It's starting to look like home, isn't it?"

Steven nodded. After classes that afternoon, he and Billie had gone on a shopping spree. They'd come back with half a dozen potted plants, a couple of big squishy throw pillows for the living-room couch, and a Chinese cooking set complete with wok, cookbook, and utensils.

Usually, Steven didn't have a lot of patience for shopping. He tended to view his sister Jessica and her friends as proof that mall cruising was a gender-linked skill. But with Billie, buying things for the apartment had actually been fun. Steven's former roommates' ideas of decorating were to throw a dozen pairs of sneakers in a closet and a frozen pizza in the oven. *Billie's different, all right*, Steven thought, laughing out loud.

Billie, who'd started chopping vegetables on a wooden cutting board, looked up. "What?" she asked, preparing to smile at whatever joke he was about to share.

"I was just thinking," Steven explained, "about the other day when I opened the door and set eyes on Billie Winkler for the very first time."

She grinned. "I wasn't what you expected, huh?"

Steven shook his head. "Hardly!" When Steven had made arrangements—all through a series of notes—with his prospective roommate, Billie, naturally he'd assumed "Billie" was a guy. "I can tell you now, I wasn't sure at first *if* it was going to work out."

Billie smiled again. "But it is working out, isn't it?"

"Yep. I couldn't have asked for a better roommate."

He headed for the refrigerator to get out the chicken, smiling at her as he went. He didn't want to gush or anything, but Billie was a fantastic roommate. She was neat, she was considerate, and she was great company. In just a few days, they'd settled into a pleasant, comfortable domestic routine—he could hardly remember what it was like before she moved in.

"No, really," Steven said. "You don't leave dirty dishes in the sink, or hog the bathroom and use up all the hot water. You have a great collection of CDs and videos, you're smart and funny . . ."

And gorgeous . . .

"Well, with all those stellar qualities I just might rent myself out as the perfect roommate!" Billie quipped. "OK," said Billie as she whisked some sauce ingredients together in a bowl. "Put the wok on the stove. We're ready to stir-fry!"

Steven watched Billie as she talked, admiring her delicate profile and the way the curtain of silky chestnut hair swept her cheek. *Not that it matters that she's gorgeous,* he told himself quickly. *She's my roomie, my buddy. We're living together—not "Living Together" living together, but living together.*

When the oil in the wok was smoking hot, Steven tossed in the vegetables and Billie quickly stirred them around with chopsticks, her eye on the clock.

Just then, the phone rang. "I'll get it," Steven offered, reaching for the receiver. "Yo," he said cheerfully into the phone, smiling at Billie, who smiled back at him.

"Steven, it's Dad," said the voice on the other end of the line.

"Dad." The smile faded from Steven's face. For a while there, he'd almost forgotten what was going on with his family. The hour's drive that separated his life at college from the tragedy in Sweet Valley had, for a brief time, seemed like a thousand miles. Now, like a tidal wave, it all rushed back over him. "How are things going?" he asked his father.

"Well, we're all a little tense about tomorrow," Mr. Wakefield admitted. "I was hoping you could spare me a few minutes—I'd like to run some things by you, get your advice."

"Of course," said Steven, glad that his father felt he could turn to him even though he wasn't a real lawyer yet himself, just a prelaw undergrad. "Umm . . ." His gaze shifted to Billie, who was still busy at the wok. The vegetables sizzled and crackled as they cooked. "Hold on a sec, Dad."

Untangling the phone cord, Steven carried the receiver out of the kitchen and into the hallway. When he was in his bedroom, he put the phone to his ear again. "I'm here, Dad," he said. "What's up?"

Mr. Wakefield proceeded to talk for five minutes straight, using his son as a sounding board. Steven got the sense that his father just needed reassurance that he was on the right track with his strategy for Elizabeth's defense.

"It sounds like you've thought of everything,"

Steven responded. "Your case is as solid as it could get . . . under the circumstances."

Mr. Wakefield sighed heavily. "Under the circumstances," he agreed.

"How's everyone holding up?" Steven asked.

"About as you'd expect. Your mom is running around the house like June Cleaver, cooking and dusting and vacuuming, and basically pretending she's a fifties housewife so she won't have time to worry. Elizabeth went straight to her room after dinner, without touching her food. She and Jessica still aren't speaking."

Steven twisted the phone cord tightly around his hand. "Gosh, I wish those two would get over this," he exclaimed. "I wish Jessica would say *something* to Liz—scream at her, *anything* rather than this punitive silent treatment."

"I guess it's going to take a little more time."

"Yeah, but there *isn't* more time," Steven pointed out. "The trial starts tomorrow. Liz needs her."

"What about you?" Mr. Wakefield asked.

"I'll be there," Steven asserted. "Of course I'll be there. You can count on me—you can both count on me."

"Thanks, son. Thanks for listening."

"Try to get some sleep, Dad. I'm coming home tonight, so I'll see you first thing in the morning."

"OK, son," his father said, and the line went

dead. Steven dropped the receiver on the bed and sat for a moment with his head in his hands. When the phone started beeping because it was off the hook, Steven rose and walked slowly back to the kitchen.

Billie was still cooking. "It's almost ready," she told Steven. "I hope you're hungry!"

He nodded. "Sure. What can I do to help?"

"You could throw a couple of place mats and some chopsticks on the table," she suggested.

A minute later, they sat down to dinner. "Yum," Billie said, tasting the stir-fried chicken and vegetables. "Pretty tasty, if I may say so myself."

Steven poked at the food. He'd lost his appetite, and even though he knew it was rude after all the trouble Billie had gone to cook for him, he couldn't bring himself to eat. Finally, he just pushed his plate away.

Concern shadowed Billie's eyes. "Sorry," Steven mumbled. "I've kind of ruined the mood here. It's just—"

"Ssh." Billie touched her finger gently and briefly to his lips. "It's OK, Steven. We don't have to talk about it. I know what you're going through."

Steven couldn't help laughing bitterly. "Thanks, Billie, but it's just not possible. You're a very empathic person, and I appreciate the way you've been such a good listener these last few days. But you just can't know what it feels like, having your kid sister on trial for manslaughter."

Billie dropped her eyes. For a moment, she was at a loss for words, just as Steven thought she'd be.

When she looked up there were tears in her eyes. "No, Steven, you're right," she said, weighing her words carefully. "I've never had a sister on trial for manslaughter. But my family has had their share of problems, as has every family, so don't make the mistake of thinking that you're alone and no one could possibly understand what you're going through."

Steven stared at her, speechless. He was astonished by Billie's words and also, in a strange way, comforted. *I'm not alone with this,* he realized. *Maybe she really* does *understand. I'm not alone.*

Wordlessly, Steven reached for Billie's hand. Billie leaned across the table, gently smoothing the hair back from his forehead and brushing the tear from his cheek.

"You want to go *where*?" Todd asked in disbelief on Monday night.

"The Beach Disco," Jessica repeated.

"You want to go dancing, on a school night, the night before . . ."

The words he didn't utter seemed to hang, visibly suspended, in the silence. *The night before Elizabeth's trial. . . .*

Jessica folded her arms across her chest, her jaw set stubbornly. "Look, you're the one who called me," she reminded him. "Why did you bother if you didn't want to do something?"

With a sigh, Todd started the BMW and pulled away from the curb in front of the Wakefields' house. Jessica had a point. *Why did I call her, anyway?* he asked himself as he drove toward the ocean. Before he realized what he was doing, he answered the question out loud. "I didn't want to be alone tonight."

Jessica turned to him, her eyes hungry and eager. "Me, either," she murmured. "When the phone rang, I was just about to call *you*."

She snuggled as close to him as she could, resting her head on his shoulder. Holding the steering wheel with one hand, Todd slipped an arm around her. *This is OK,* he told himself, fighting down the feelings of guilt. *We just want to distract ourselves from our troubles—we're just keeping each other company. What's wrong with that?*

A short while later, as he and Jessica hit the open-air dance floor at the Beach Disco, a popular Sweet Valley teen hangout, Todd almost started to believe his own rationalizations. The music was lively and fun and Jessica was a great partner, setting a pace that kept him breathless. "This is a serious workout—better than basketball practice!" he joked.

Jessica grabbed his hands and twirled him in a circle. "Isn't it great therapy?" she shouted over the music. "Doesn't it make you feel free?"

One song pounded into the next with no intermission, and Todd and Jessica kept moving. *It is great therapy*, Todd decided. *That's what it is— that's all it is.* They weren't doing anything outrageous, being together like this. He'd fast-danced with Jessica a million times in the past; she was his girlfriend's sister, after all. *Except she's not "my girlfriend's sister" anymore, because Liz isn't my girlfriend*, Todd corrected himself. *So that makes her . . .*

Abruptly, the song he and Jessica were dancing to faded into something new. The tempo downshifted; the beat became pulsing and slow. Jessica's eyes locked onto Todd's and she drew closer to him, wrapping her arms around his waist, her body swaying seductively.

Any illusions Todd might have had about this being a harmless, platonic evening flew out the window. He was holding Jessica in his arms—the moment couldn't be more romantic. And the worst part was he was enjoying himself. This wasn't playtime; this wasn't "therapy."

My God, how can we be doing this? he wondered as Jessica raised her face to his, her eyes glowing as soft and bright as the stars overhead. *Tonight of all nights?* Todd's feet faltered and even though Jessica's body was warm against his, he shuddered as if from a sudden chill. *We might as well be dancing on Sam's grave,* he realized. And Elizabeth . . .

"Kiss me," Jessica whispered, her arms tightening around him.

Obediently, Todd bent his head, pressing his lips lightly against hers. He intended the kiss to be brief, but somehow he found his mouth lingering on Jessica's. The slow passion of the music seemed to hold them together, melding their bodies into one. The kiss grew deeper, and longer. . . . Finally, Todd abandoned himself to it. The kiss was tangible and real, something they both could feel and understand—something to hold on to in all the heartbreaking confusion that swirled around them.

Wrapped in her bathrobe, Elizabeth sat at her desk with pen in hand and her journal open before her. *If I could just write,* she thought, staring at the empty page, *I know it would make me feel better. Put down a few words,* she instructed herself. *Say anything!*

But her hand remained frozen; the page re-

45

mained blank. For almost as long as she could remember, this journal had been her constant, faithful companion, providing solace and relief in times of stress and heartache. But the trouble she was in now . . . even her love of writing seemed to wither and die in the face of it.

Tossing the pen down, Elizabeth jumped to her feet. For a few minutes, she paced the bedroom, her body surging with pent-up nervous energy. She was tempted to throw on some sweats and go jogging, but it was dark and late—almost midnight. *If only I had some one to talk to . . .*

She thought first of Todd, and then of Jessica. Shoving both images from her mind, Elizabeth stepped out into the hallway. *Mom,* she decided. *I need my mother.*

She had a hunch her father at least would still be up, preparing for tomorrow's trial. Tiptoeing downstairs, Elizabeth spied him at the kitchen table, hunched over a law book.

The sound of the TV drew Elizabeth to the den. A black-and-white movie flickered on the screen, but Mrs. Wakefield wasn't watching it. Instead, she stood by the bookshelves, taking volumes down one by one to dust them.

As Elizabeth entered the room, Mrs. Wakefield glanced up in surprise. "Honey, what are you doing up so late?"

46

"I'm . . . I'm . . ." Not able to find the words, Elizabeth waited for her mother to do something—to say something comforting, to walk over to her and fold her in a warm, maternal embrace. When Mrs. Wakefield didn't speak or move, tears sprang to Elizabeth's eyes. "Mom," she whispered. "I'm scared."

Mrs. Wakefield gave the book a quick flick with the feather duster and returned it to the shelf. As she headed for the door to the hall, she patted Elizabeth's shoulder in passing. "You'll do fine," she said brightly, as if Elizabeth were just seeking a little encouragement before a big test. "Get a good night's sleep, and we'll have a big breakfast in the morning!"

Her vision blurred by tears, Elizabeth stared after her mother's retreating figure. *Don't go*, she wanted to cry. *I need you. Don't leave me alone.*

But she choked back the words. *She was never really here*, Elizabeth recognized. *I was alone before she even left the room.* The tears flowed faster, spilling down her cheeks in two hot streams. *Alone . . .*

Bet I'm the first one up, Steven thought on Tuesday morning as he swung his legs over the side of his bed at the Wakefield house and stuck his feet into his slippers. His alarm wouldn't go off for another hour; it was still dark outside. There was no point lying around any longer, though—he'd tossed and turned all night, unable to grab more than a few minutes' sleep.

I'll make the most of it. I'll cook breakfast for everybody, Steven decided as he shuffled downstairs. *Billie's special pancakes will be just the thing to get us ready for this ordeal.*

As he approached the kitchen, however, his nose informed him that someone was already at work there. Mrs. Wakefield, wearing a slim navy suit and cream-colored silk blouse, stood at the stove, sautéeing vegetables in a skillet. *Did she even go to bed at all?* Steven wondered.

"Morning, Mom," he greeted her.

Mrs. Wakefield waved a spatula at him. "Hi, hon. You're a little early, but I'll have a hot meal ready for you in a jiffy." She recited the menu. "Sausage and vegetable frittata, homemade blueberry bran muffins, cantaloupe, fresh-squeezed OJ, fresh-brewed coffee . . . How does that sound?"

"Delicious," said Steven. "Thanks for going to all the trouble. I know you can't feel much like cooking."

"Oh, I think it's so important that we all eat right and keep our strength up," she replied, cracking some eggs into the skillet. "Little things can be big morale boosters. I was telling your father just last night, 'Don't underestimate the importance of choosing the right tie.'"

Steven looked blank. "The right tie?"

"The right necktie," Mrs. Wakefield explained. "You know, if you wear the right clothes, not only do you *look* more powerful and capable, you *feel* more powerful and capable."

"Well, uh, sure," Steven stuttered.

"It could make all the difference to his confidence with a case this marginal," commented Mrs. Wakefield. Opening the oven, she checked the muffins. "Let's give them another minute or two, shall we?"

"Yeah, OK." A sick feeling in his stomach, Steven watched his mother bustle around the kitchen. *A case this marginal? How can she talk that way?* He wanted to grab her shoulders and shake her, startle her into facing up to reality. *But she'd probably just tell me to go to my room and polish my shoes or something,* he thought. *This must be some kind of radical defense mechanism. She's just going through the motions—she's blacking out on what's really happening.*

But even as he reached this conclusion, Steven knew that *he* wasn't facing up to reality, either. He couldn't simply analyze it away. He hoped there wasn't something seriously wrong with his mother. . . .

Chapter 4

It's time, Elizabeth thought, staring out the car window at the Sweet Valley County Courthouse as her father parked. She clutched the pocketbook she held on her lap, her fingernails digging into the leather. *I have to get out of the car and walk up that sidewalk and through the door and stand trial.*

She didn't know if she could do it. Suddenly Elizabeth's whole body felt numb and cold. *I can't move. I feel like a dead person.* The image of Sam Woodruff's face flashed through her mind. Dead.

"Elizabeth."

At the sound of her mother's voice, Elizabeth blinked. Alice Wakefield had twisted around in the

51

front seat to gaze at her daughter. "Honey, are you ready?" she asked quietly.

Elizabeth licked her lips, which were as dry as paper. "Yes," she whispered. "I'm ready."

Steven, sitting next to Elizabeth in the backseat, reached over and squeezed her hand. "It's going to be OK," he told her. "We'll be with you all the way." His words, meant to be comforting, only reminded Elizabeth that they *weren't* all with her. Her very own twin sister was very much against her, and conspicuously absent this morning.

Mr. Wakefield climbed out of the driver's seat and walked around to open the car door for his daughter. Taking a deep breath, Elizabeth stepped out onto the pavement.

A small crowd of people had already gathered on the steps of the courthouse. As the Wakefields approached, they turned. Elizabeth heard the buzz of excited voices. Before she knew what was happening, the reporters pressed forward, holding out microphones and aiming cameras.

"Miss Wakefield, will you take the stand in your own defense?" "Has your memory returned, Miss Wakefield?" "Mr. Wakefield, is it true you fired your daughter's attorney because he considered this case unwinnable and pressured you to plea-bargain?" "Miss Wakefield, wasn't the victim your twin sister's boyfriend?"

The horrible questions rained down like hailstones and Elizabeth felt herself cower under their barrage.

Ned Wakefield wrapped one arm protectively around Elizabeth's shoulders. Raising the other arm, he shielded her from the reporters' eager eyes. "No comment," he snapped, hustling her through the wide double doors into the lobby of the courthouse.

But there was no escaping the scrutiny of the public. Dozens of people milled about inside, and they weren't all reporters, Elizabeth saw. Many were just curious bystanders, drawn by a sensational story. Elizabeth dropped her eyes to the floor, wishing she were invisible. She felt sick to her stomach. *They've come to see me. They've come to look at a murderer.*

Flanked by her parents and Steven, Elizabeth entered the courtroom. With relief, she sank into a seat next to her father at a long, narrow table in front. The courtroom was packed full, but at least the crowd was behind her—she didn't have to face them.

Mr. Wakefield approached the bench, as did the district attorney who was arguing the case against her. Elizabeth watched the judge and the two lawyers converse in low tones. *It's like a made-for-TV* movie, she thought, feeling dazed and helpless. *It's a movie and I've been assigned a part, but I don't have a script. I don't know anyone's lines. I don't know what's going to happen.*

Judge Baird, a silver-haired woman in her sixties, struck her desk with a gavel. The sound echoed ominously throughout the courtroom; Elizabeth's heart jumped. Instantly, an expectant hush fell over the audience. "Court is now in session," the judge pronounced.

Elizabeth willed herself to relax as the first witness, an older man who had been the first to arrive at the scene of the crash, was called to the stand. But she couldn't keep her heart from beating double time. In just a few minutes, it would be her turn. . . .

A few quick questions established that the man had not observed the accident itself, but had driven up right after it occurred. He stepped down and Elizabeth closed her eyes, mentally preparing herself. *This is it. . . .*

"The prosecution calls Elizabeth Wakefield to the stand."

Elizabeth put her hands, cold with sweat, on the arms of her chair. She turned to her father and he smiled tightly at her. "Go ahead, sweetheart. You'll do fine."

Slowly, Elizabeth rose to her feet. She walked forward unsteadily. Her knees were shaking and she could feel her fear coursing through her veins.

"Raise your right hand," the bailiff instructed.

Trembling, Elizabeth raised her hand.

"Do you solemnly swear that you will tell the truth, the whole truth, and nothing but the truth?" he demanded.

Elizabeth opened her mouth to speak, but no sound came out. For a moment, she was afraid she might burst into tears. Then she remembered her father sitting behind her, and her mother and Steven behind him. *I have to be strong for them*, she thought, and pulled herself together the best she could. "Yes, I do," she said clearly.

The bailiff directed her toward the stand and Elizabeth lowered herself gingerly into the chair. As she looked out over the courtroom, she shuddered involuntarily. A sea of faces confronted her. All at once, she felt naked and exposed. *But they're not all strangers*, Elizabeth reminded herself. She saw her mother and Steven, and Enid, and . . .

Elizabeth's heart jumped into her throat. Todd was sitting next to Enid.

For a split second, Elizabeth felt herself buoyed up on a wave of hope. *He came. He's forgiven me!* Just as quickly, though, she plunged back into an abyss of despair. Todd's handsome face was frozen, unreadable. *He probably just wanted to see for himself*, Elizabeth thought. *This way there won't be any doubt left in his mind that I'm guilty and that he's much better off without me. . . .*

Elizabeth's gaze shifted, searching out one more face, even though she knew she wouldn't find it. Her parents had gotten permission for Jessica to miss school that day, but Jessica had refused to come to court. Still, Elizabeth scanned the courtroom. After seeing for herself that her twin sister really wasn't there, she lost control of her emotions. For the first time that morning a single tear rolled down her cheek.

Elizabeth had never felt so alone in her life when Mr. Dilworth, the prosecuting attorney, took up his position in front of her and fixed a cool, intent gaze on her face. "Miss Wakefield," he began. "Tell us what happened on the night of . . ."

Leave her alone! Todd wanted to shout. *Stop badgering her! Who does this bum Dilworth think he is, talking to Elizabeth like that? Can't he see how much she's hurting?*

But Todd knew he had to restrain himself. This was a court of law—Hempstead Dilworth wasn't a bum, he was a district attorney doing his job. Elizabeth *was* on trial, and for a very serious crime. Todd clenched his fists, swallowing hard.

"So, Elizabeth," Mr. Dilworth resumed, pacing in front the witness stand. "Did you start drinking at the prom, or had you been drinking before you went to the dance?"

Elizabeth shook her head. "I—I wasn't drinking at the prom," she stammered. "I mean, I don't remember drinking anything alcoholic. Just—just punch."

"Rum punch," the prosecutor said.

Mr. Wakefield lifted a hand. "Objection. There's no evidence that Elizabeth was drinking rum punch at the dance. Move to strike."

The judge nodded assent. Mr. Dilworth shrugged. "Withdrawn. Rum punch or no, Elizabeth, you were legally intoxicated at the time of the accident. Where did you get the liquor? Did you bring it with you to the dance? Did Sam?"

"No," said Elizabeth, wrinkling her forehead. "*I* definitely didn't, and I'm sure Sam didn't, either."

"Who gave it to you, then?"

"I . . . I don't know," Elizabeth confessed. "I don't remember *anybody* giving it to me."

The prosecutor didn't let up. "How many drinks did you have before you left the dance?" he pressed.

"I don't know," Elizabeth repeated. Todd watched as she lifted a hand to her throat and fidgeted nervously with her gold necklace. "I don't remember having any drinks."

"You don't remember having any drinks, but

you were drunk when you left the dance," the prosecutor observed. "Where were you going in the Jeep? To acquire more alcohol?"

Todd had wondered himself the night of the dance. Why was Elizabeth behaving so outrageously? What was going on between her and Sam? Why did they leave the dance together? But now he was furious at the lawyer's tone, his insinuations. How dare he?

Next to him, Todd felt Enid stiffen. He took her hand, squeezing it. Enid turned to him, her eyes wide with agony. "I can't stand this," she whispered. "How long is it going to go on?"

The relentless questioning continued. "You don't remember where you were going, but you must have been in a hurry to get there," Mr. Dilworth remarked dryly. "How fast were you driving when you lost control of the vehicle?"

"I don't know," Elizabeth replied.

"Thirty miles per hour?" he prompted. "Forty? Sixty?"

"I . . . don't . . . know," Elizabeth repeated, a quaver in her voice.

With each brutally blunt question and each feeble response, Todd's heart grew heavier and heavier. Face-to-face with Elizabeth's torment, seeing with his own eyes what the strain of the past few weeks had done to her, he suddenly found himself troubled by his own guilt.

What about me? Todd asked himself silently. *Have I done anything to help her or have I just added to her misery?* He didn't have to think about it very hard; the answer was too clear. He'd turned his back on Elizabeth completely. He'd let his own pain prevent him from feeling hers.

He recalled the moment when he'd looked down from the stage in the gym where he'd just been crowned King of the Jungle Prom. There on the dance floor were Elizabeth and Sam with their arms around each other, hugging and kissing. He'd been terribly hurt and angry. He hadn't known they'd been drinking, but he *had* known that betraying him—and with her sister's boyfriend no less—was wildly uncharacteristic behavior for Elizabeth. *But I never even tried to find out what it meant. And after the accident I didn't even let her explain. Maybe I shouldn't have even needed an explanation. Maybe a guy should just be there for the girl he loves.*

Todd stared at Elizabeth, a wave of guilt and self-loathing washing over him. *Yeah. Maybe a guy should be there for his girlfriend instead of turning around and dating her twin sister.* Todd's broad shoulders slumped as he thought about Jessica and remembered the other night at the beach. *What on earth was I doing?*

The prosecutor wrapped up a round of questions, and then it was Mr. Wakefield's turn. It was clear to Todd that Elizabeth's father was doing his best to present his daughter's situation in a sympathetic light, but it was equally clear that his argument on her behalf was painfully thin. She couldn't remember anything about the circumstances of the car crash, so she had absolutely nothing to say in her own defense. And the only other person who was with her at the time was dead.

Each passing minute felt like an hour to Todd as his nerves stretched tighter and tighter. When court finally adjourned for the day, he popped up from his seat like a jack-in-the-box.

Enid's eyes were on Elizabeth, who was standing with her family at the front of the room. "I'm going to wait for her," Enid told Todd.

There was a hint of a question in Enid's voice. Todd hesitated, split down the middle by conflicting impulses. He realized now how incredibly selfish he'd been, punishing Elizabeth this way. He wanted so much to go to her, to comfort her, to hold her. . . . *But what right do I have, after turning my back on her ever since the accident?* he wondered unhappily. *What would I say? I can't approach her here, of all places, in front of all these people. . . .*

"I think I'm going to head back to school,"

Todd muttered. "I can probably make it to my last class."

Before Enid could reply, Todd melted into the crowd pouring out of the courtroom. His heart was aching to be with Elizabeth, but he couldn't face her—not yet.

As Jessica watched Todd pick at his slice of pepperoni pizza, she could barely conceal her annoyance. She knew why he was so preoccupied and in such a crummy mood. *He went to the trial today,* she thought to herself, not even wanting to consider what that might mean.

Jessica pushed her plate away, her own appetite vanishing. "Well, I can't eat, either," she said snappishly. "Let's just have this wrapped and get out of here."

Five minutes later, they were walking across the parking lot of Guido's Pizza Palace. When they reached Todd's BMW, he opened the passenger door for Jessica. "I'm sorry," he mumbled, not meeting her eyes. "I guess I'm not the best company tonight. Why don't I just take you home?"

"No," Jessica said quickly. She sensed that if she let Todd leave her now, she might lose her fragile hold over him—he might slip through her fingers forever. *If he's alone, he'll just think about her. . . .* "No," Jessica repeated, placing a hand on Todd's arm and gazing up at him with wide, appealing eyes. "I don't want to go home yet. It's too depressing—I can't deal with it. Let's go for a drive, OK?"

Todd shrugged. Jessica tucked herself into the car and he slammed the door after her, then walked around to slip behind the wheel. "Buckle up, OK?" he said gruffly, starting the engine with a roar.

Jessica fastened her safety belt. An unwanted thought flashed through her mind. *Sam wasn't wearing a seat belt that night. Maybe if he had, he wouldn't be . . .*

Todd pointed the car toward the ocean and they drove in silence, each lost in their thoughts.

The last orange glimmer of sunset was fading from the western horizon as the BMW coasted to a stop in the deserted beachfront parking lot. Todd turned off the engine, but made no move to get out of the car. Instead, he sat stiffly, his hands still gripping the steering wheel.

He looks like a statue, cold and untouchable, Jessica thought. *He doesn't want to be with me,* she realized with a sickening lurch of her stomach. *He's not even trying to pretend anymore.*

She wanted to cry, to yell, to shake him until any memories of Elizabeth were erased from his brain. Breathing slowly and deeply, she held herself together with an effort. "Todd," she said softly after a moment, "what's the matter?"

With a sigh, Todd dropped his hands from the wheel and sank back in his seat. "I'm sorry, Jess," he replied. "I'm just feeling a little . . . confused."

Jessica detected the note of uncertainty and vulnerability in his voice and hastened to exploit it. "Confused?" She slid closer to him, her shoulder brushing against his. "Why?" she asked, even though she was pretty sure she knew. She kept her voice gentle, caressing. "What about?"

"About . . . you," Todd confessed. "About Liz. Being out with you like this—it just feels wrong. Especially tonight, after the first day of her trial." His jaw clenched. "When I saw what they were putting her through . . ."

"What *they* were putting her through? Todd, she did this to herself," Jessica reminded him. "No one else is guilty."

Todd shook his head. "I don't know about that. *I* feel guilty."

"That's crazy," Jessica insisted. "You're not guilty of anything."

"I can't help the way I feel," Todd burst out, his voice cracking.

"Yes, you can," Jessica told him, slipping her arm through his, pressing closer. "*I* can help you. It's OK for us to be together, Todd. It's the right thing, not the wrong thing."

When Todd didn't answer, she had to struggle to subdue her impatience. Why did he cling so stubbornly to his attachment to Elizabeth? Couldn't he see that Jessica was the one he was meant to be with? Hadn't they secretly been drawn to each other from the very beginning? *We would have been going steady ages ago, if Liz hadn't stolen him away from me,* Jessica reflected. *I won't let her take him away from me again. She already took Sam away. I won't be left alone, with nothing.*

"Don't you see?" Jessica whispered urgently. "It's just you and me now, Todd, right down the line. *She* did this. *Elizabeth* did this. No matter what she says . . ." Jessica's voice shook with emotion. "No matter what she says, it won't change the fact that Sam is dead and that she took him away that night. She left us both, Todd. *She* left *us*, not the other way around."

Jessica lifted a hand to Todd's face, brushing away the tear that trickled down his cheek. He turned blindly toward her, and she kissed him, gently at first and then more passionately as he began to respond to her. "See?" she whispered, wrapping her arms around his waist. "It's just you and me."

Chapter 5

"You didn't have to do this, you know," Steven said to Billie on Tuesday night as they slid into a booth at the Dairi Burger. "I mean, drive all the way down here, and on a weeknight."

"It was no big deal," Billie assured him. "I got the feeling when you called that you could use some company." She smiled playfully. "Hey, any excuse not to work on that physics problem set!"

"Well, I really appreciate it," Steven told her. "I love my family, and I want to be there for them, but I needed a break, you know?"

She nodded sympathetically. "It must have been a rough day for all of you."

"I had to get out of the house for a while,"

Steven admitted. "Jessica split, too. God knows where she went or who she's with, though—she never tells anybody. I just hope she's not alone. I hope she has a friend . . . like I do." Reaching out, Steven squeezed Billie's hand. "Thanks," he said quietly.

"Anytime."

They gazed silently into each other's eyes and, without warning, a new and powerful emotion flickered in Steven's heart. Suddenly he didn't care if he never let go of Billie's hand, if he never pulled himself from the warm, deep pool of her eyes.

Finally, she broke the spell herself, her cheeks pink. "What are roomies for, right?" she said lightly. "Hey, let's order some food—I'm starving."

Soon they were digging into grilled-chicken sandwiches, onion rings, and a couple of the Dairi Burger's famous shakes, thankful for the distraction. "Excuse me for gobbling," Billie said with her mouth full, "but it's been a long time since lunch."

"And you played soccer this afternoon, didn't you?" Steven asked, happy to ease back into their comfortable patter.

"Yep." She grinned. "Your team missed you, Wakefield. We tanned your hides, six to two."

"Ouch." Steven winced. "But don't get cocky, Winkler. We play you again in a couple weeks, and I guarantee we'll have you begging for mercy."

66

"I'll believe it when I see it," she said. "Oh, by the way, what's-her-name, Eve, said to tell you the prelaw study group is meeting tomorrow night instead of tonight."

"Great," said Steven. "My poli-sci class this semester is intense—I'd be lost if I didn't get the chance to talk over the reading material with those guys."

He and Billie sat, eating and chatting, for over an hour. It wasn't any different from the countless meals they had shared before. The only hint that anything unusual had passed between them was the pink glow still visible in Billie's cheeks.

When they stood up to leave, he slung an arm companionably around Billie's slender shoulders. "You were just what the doctor ordered," he told her. "I feel about a million percent better."

"Glad to hear it." She hugged him around the waist as they walked toward the exit. "So, while I've got you in such a good mood, how about knocking a hundred bucks or so off my monthly rent?"

"Hey, I'm grateful, not stupid!"

Laughing, they pushed through the door . . . nearly walking right into Elizabeth.

"Liz!" Steven exclaimed in surprise. For a short while, he'd almost forgotten about his family's troubles. Seeing Elizabeth, alone and clearly holding herself together with supreme effort, brought it all back. Guilt-stricken, Steven pulled his arm away from Billie. "What are *you* doing here?"

Elizabeth gave her brother a forced, hollow smile. "I'm a big girl, Steven," she reminded him. "I can go out at night if I want. Besides, I've got to start living my life again sometime."

She attempted another smile, but it wasn't convincing. Steven stared at her helplessly, wishing he knew what to say or do to make things easier for her.

Billie eased gracefully into the awkward silence. "You know," she encouraged Elizabeth. "You should come up and visit us on campus sometime. It would be a change of scenery, and we'd have fun—playing tennis, cooking dinner, short-sheeting Steven's bed. . . ."

This time, Elizabeth's smile was genuine; Steven could almost see her relax. "Maybe I will," she said.

"What are you doing now?" Billie asked. "Want to join us for a movie?"

The haunted, defensive look returned to Elizabeth's eyes. "No, thanks. I—I've got to do this by myself." She pulled her shoulders up. "I think I should get used to being on my own. So long, guys."

Steven watched Elizabeth enter the restaurant,

fighting the urge to run after her, to shield her from the gossip and the curious, insensitive eyes he knew she'd have to face inside. He felt his throat choke with tears.

Billie was watching him steadily. "She'll be OK," she predicted, placing a comforting hand on Steven's arm. "She's strong. Now *you* have to be strong, too—for her sake."

"I know, but sometimes it's hard. God, it's so hard." All at once, Steven thought that if he didn't pour it all out, he'd burst. He had to tell someone what he was dealing with, the full horror of the situation at home: not only did Elizabeth face the very real possibility of being sent to a juvenile detention home, but his mother was teetering on the edge of a nervous breakdown. He had to tell someone. He had to tell Billie. He just couldn't carry the burden by himself anymore.

"There's something I have to talk to you about, Billie," Steven whispered. "I swore to myself I wouldn't tell anyone, though, so you have to promise—promise you'll keep it a secret."

He searched her face with urgent, desperate eyes. She looked back at him, her own eyes clear and warm with concern and affection. "I won't tell a soul. You can trust me," Billie told him, and Steven knew he could.

❊   ❊   ❊

Pamela sat slumped in a booth at the Dairi Burger, a burger and fries sitting untouched on the plate in front of her. She'd been at the restaurant for half an hour and kids were constantly walking in and out, but so far nobody had made the slightest move to approach her. She hadn't received a single hello or even a nod of recognition.

This is definitely the place to go if you want to see and be seen in Sweet Valley. Too bad I'm invisible! Pamela thought with glum irony.

Wistfully, she stole glances at a group of kids sitting nearby. They talked and laughed with that relaxed, unself-conscious manner of people who belonged. *Those girls look so carefree and confident. What I wouldn't give to be like that.*

She sipped her soda, her gaze wandering until it came to rest on one other person who didn't fit into the high-spirited, congenial scene. Elizabeth Wakefield had just walked in, alone.

She looked as lonely as Pamela felt. Like Pamela, Elizabeth's reputation preceded her, only hers was a little more positive. Even at Big Mesa, everyone knew that Elizabeth Wakefield was one of the nicest kids at Sweet Valley High—friendly and unpretentious. *The kind of person who'd give you the benefit of the doubt instead of judging you on what other people said about you,* Pamela reflected. *The kind of person I'd like to be friends with . . . .*

Hey, maybe it's not such a crazy idea, Pamela thought. *Maybe Elizabeth Wakefield needs someone to talk to as much as I do.* No one else was making a move to go up to Elizabeth, that was for sure. Pamela took a deep breath, mustering all her courage. She'd do it—she'd go up to Elizabeth and introduce herself and invite her to sit down. . . .

Too late. A take-out bag clutched in her hand, Elizabeth hurried back to the door, with her white face and limp hair looking like nothing so much as a frightened ghost.

With a sigh, Pamela reached into her shoulder bag and pulled out a copy of the Sweet Valley High student newspaper, *The Oracle.* Flipping it open, she skimmed the articles until she came to a calendar of weekly meetings and activities. *I can't give up on my new school yet—I've got to get involved somehow,* she decided, considering the possibilities. Photography club? Drama club? The tennis team?

At that moment, Pamela looked up and caught the eye of a boy just entering the restaurant. Her face turned scarlet, his turned white and cold.

Bruce hesitated, but only for an instant. Regaining his self-command, he swaggered across to the new take-out counter, Ronnie Edwards and Paul Sherwood following in his wake.

Bruce didn't give Pamela another glance.

71

Ronnie and Paul, meanwhile, leered in her direction, Ronnie making some remark under his breath that caused Paul to laugh loudly. Pamela cringed, not sure which was worse, being ignored by Bruce or being ridiculed by his friends.

She'd dreamed of bumping into Bruce here, of getting a chance to talk to him and straighten things out. But now, as Bruce and his buddies waited at the take-out counter for their food, and people at other tables directed amused, disdainful looks her way, Pamela prayed that Bruce would just leave.

After what seemed like an eternity, Bruce sauntered back out of the Dairi Burger, still without acknowledging her presence. Fighting back tears of hurt and humiliation, Pamela counted to twenty-five in her head. When she figured Bruce had time to clear out and it was safe to venture into the parking lot, she slipped from her booth and bolted for the door just as her eyes brimmed over.

Elizabeth sat at the desk in her bedroom staring at a neat stack of unopened schoolbooks. It was almost eleven P.M. Back in the old days, she would've been getting ready for bed—putting on her nightgown, brushing her teeth, eager to fall into bed exhausted after a full day. But she knew there was no point in going through that routine

72

tonight, at least not for a while. Lately, she put it off as long as she could. Why hurry to bed when she knew she wouldn't fall asleep—she'd just lie there, staring at the shadowy ceiling, thinking. And her thoughts were so much harder to bear after the lights went out, when she was left alone, in the dark. . . .

This wasn't such a bad night, though, Elizabeth reflected with a tiny flicker of optimism. She was proud of herself for going to the Dairi Burger earlier that evening, for getting out and facing Sweet Valley even though she knew everyone from school—everyone in town, for that matter—was talking about her. It was the first time she'd ventured out in ages, except to go to court, and it hadn't been fun. But she'd survived.

Pulling a textbook toward her, Elizabeth opened it up to the chapter Enid had marked with a scrap of paper. Every afternoon, Enid stopped by with Elizabeth's homework assignments. Elizabeth was determined to stay on top of her work so that she wouldn't be hopelessly behind her classmates when she returned to Sweet Valley High. *Make that if I return to Sweet Valley High. If by some miracle I'm not convicted and sent to a juvenile reformatory. . . .*

She snapped the book shut. It was no use. How could she concentrate on biology when she might never again set foot in the halls of Sweet Valley High, might never see graduation day, never go on to college, never have a career as a writer, never realize any of the dreams she'd cherished over the years?

Elizabeth pushed back her chair and looked slowly around her bedroom. All at once, everything there—each piece of furniture, every little knick-knack—seemed unspeakably precious. She tried not to think about the room she'd live in at the reformatory, but she couldn't help picturing it—a barren cell, devoid of color and comfort, with no feeling of security, no privacy, no reminders of her happy childhood. . . .

Standing up, Elizabeth walked to her nightstand and picked up a small silver picture frame. It held a photograph of herself and Todd, taken at a party at Ken Matthews's house just a few months ago. Maria Santelli had taken it, and in it Elizabeth and Todd were laughing—Winston had been telling some typically hilarious story. Todd had his arm around Elizabeth's shoulders and they were laughing. . . .

We look so happy, Elizabeth thought, smiling through a mist of tears. "Oh, Todd," she whispered out loud. "I miss those days. I miss you."

She put the frame down and sat on the edge of the bed. Opening the nightstand drawer, she pulled out a small leather-bound photo album. Elizabeth turned to the familiar scrawl on the inside of the front cover. "See, Liz? We're the dynamic duo! Since we were only born four minutes apart, we should never let anything come between us. Let's make up. Love, Jess." That was just like Jessica, Elizabeth mused, smiling sadly to herself. Manipulating me to get me to forgive her. Jessica had put this album together after they'd had a particularly bad fight, filling it with especially meaningful pictures of the twins together.

The first snapshot was of Elizabeth and Jessica in diapers and tiny Santa Claus hats, posed in front of the tree on their first Christmas morning. In the next picture, they were at the beach and a little older, wearing matching ruffled bathing suits and carrying plastic pails and shovels. *And here we are on our first day of kindergarten,* Elizabeth reminisced, *and at Grandma and Grandpa's in Michigan.* Turning the page, she burst out laughing at a photo of her and Jessica dressed in bobby socks, poodle skirts, and cardigans worn backward for a middle school sock hop.

In the last picture, the twins were standing with their arms around each other preparing to blow out the candles on the cake at their Sweet Sixteen birthday party. A solitary tear stole down Elizabeth's cheek. *We were always so close,* she thought, reaching for a tissue. *I'll miss her so much. But she'll be better off without me. Without me around to remind her of the tragedy, she can get over it and get on with her life. . . .*

Elizabeth walked slowly around her room, stopping to touch and examine some of her more treasured possessions: a turquoise and silver bracelet Todd had brought back for her from his last article she'd written for *The Oracle*; a picture of her parents on their wedding day; a book of poems Enid had given her; a threadbare stuffed rabbit she'd owned since babyhood. Some of the items made her cry a little, but others brought a smile to her face. *Most of my memories are so very, very happy. . . .*

At that moment, Elizabeth spotted something pushed far back on the top of her dresser—the crumpled corsage that had still been pinned to her prom dress when they pulled her . . . and Sam . . . from the wreckage of the Jeep.

Elizabeth clutched the faded flowers, crushing them. The ocean of pain she'd been keeping bottled up inside suddenly burst from her. "Oh, God, what have I done?" she moaned, a terrible, anguished sob tearing at her throat. Burying her face in her hands, she fell on her bed, choking with grief.

"Lincolnville," the bus driver's voice crackled

over the loudspeaker, waking Margo, who had fallen asleep staring dully out the bus window at the black, star-filled night. "We'll take a fifteen-minute rest stop here, folks."

What a treat, Margo thought disdainfully as she stepped out onto the sidewalk a minute later. She lifted a hand to protect her eyes from the gritty wind that stirred a few fallen leaves in the gutter. *Another dirty, deadbeat prairie town that could be wiped off the map and nobody would miss it.*

Slinging her pocketbook over her shoulder, she sauntered at a leisurely pace toward the neon lights of a ramshackle variety store halfway down the block. A bell jingled as she stepped through the door. Ignoring the inquiring glance of a skinny, pimple-faced boy working behind the counter, Margo wandered over to the magazine rack. First, with an insolent snap of her bubble gum, she lifted out a copy of *Sweet Sixteen*, flipping idly through the glossy pages. Then she scanned the newspapers. Would any of them mention the incidents in Ohio, the jewelry theft or the "accidental" drowning of little Georgie? Had anyone made a connection between the two, or between Georgie's death and the death of Margo's foster sister in the fire on Long Island? Had they found the common denominator?

Casually, Margo reached for the Chicago paper.

She skimmed the headlines: nothing. The St. Louis paper also revealed nothing.

Margo struggled to keep a smug, self-satisfied grin from her face. *I got away with it!* she thought jubilantly.

"May I help you, miss?" a voice croaked behind her.

Margo spun on her heel to find the boy at the counter standing right behind her. *The idiot snuck up on me!* she thought, her temper flaring. *What's he doing, spying on me?*

"I don't need help," she snapped, replacing the newspaper with a quick, violent gesture.

The young man wrung his hands in dismay as if he feared what Margo would say next. Margo caught herself, resisting the urge to tell him just how repulsive he was, shove past him, and exit the store. With a concentrated effort, she transmuted her scowl into a sweetly apologetic smile.

"I am *so* sorry," Margo said. "You see, I've been riding on a bus all the way from the East Coast and I'm just so tired and grouchy, I can't stand my own company! Those buses sure don't do anything for your disposition. There's no excuse, though, for taking it out on you when you were being so nice. I hope you'll forgive me."

The boy's face relaxed instantly. "Oh, don't worry," he said in a warm, hopeful tone. "You just go right on and enjoy your shopping."

Margo sighed ruefully. "I'm not shopping, really," she confessed. "Just looking. I'm pretty hungry and bored, but money's awful tight at this point in the trip. I spent all my savings traveling out to visit with my grandmother before she . . ." Margo squeezed a tear into her eye. "Before she passed on," she finished with a delicate sniffle.

The young man looked terrified at the prospect of Margo crying in his store. "I'm sorry. Here." He took a copy of *Sweet Sixteen* and handed it to her. Then he quickly crossed to the counter and reached for a paper bag, which he filled with candy and snacks. "And take these."

"Oh, no, I couldn't—" Margo protested.

"Go on." He pressed the bag into Margo's free hand and waved her toward the door.

The driver pulled the door closed as soon as Margo jumped on board. The bus huffed forward and Margo collapsed into her seat. Unwrapping a candy bar, she bit into it with a smile, thinking how much better it tasted because she'd gotten it for free.

It's getting easier and easier, she reflected. *There's nobody I can't fool!* She wanted to laugh out loud. She wanted to tell the other passengers on the bus; it seemed such a shame to keep her triumph to herself. But of course, keeping her skills a secret was the only way she could succeed.

And she *would* succeed—no doubt about it. Just as she'd anticipated, no one seemed to be following her. So far, she'd gotten away with everything—the theft, the murders . . . she was invincible!

And I'm getting closer to Sweet Valley every minute, Margo mused, relishing the thought of the miles rolling away under the wheels of the bus. *And then the real fun begins.*

Chapter 6

The door swung open just as Todd was lifting his hand to ring the bell of Steven's apartment on Wednesday afternoon. A beautiful girl in faded jeans and a tank top breezed out, nearly walking right into him.

"Whoa, sorry!" she apologized, tossing back her chestnut hair and smiling up at him. "Are you here to see Steven? I'm his roommate, Billie. Hey, Steven!" she yelled back over her shoulder. "It's—"

"Todd," he supplied.

"Todd's here!" Billie adjusted her backpack, then gave Todd a friendly wave. "So long. Nice meeting you."

Todd laughed. "Nice meeting you, too!"

Steven had appeared at the door. "Hey, Todd, good to see you. Come on in."

Todd stepped into the living room. "Wow, this place is great," he commented. "And did I just hear that girl say she's your *roommate*?"

Steven grinned. "It's not what you think. She was the first person to answer my ad, and she just happened to be female, that's all. But what's up with you? What brings you up this way?"

While Steven grabbed a couple of cans of soda from the refrigerator, Todd sat down on the sofa and considered how to answer. He decided he should just get to the point. "It's about Elizabeth. I was hoping you could give me some advice," he told Steven.

Steven handed him a can, then pulled up a chair. "I get the impression you two aren't on the best terms these days."

Todd sighed. "Yeah, well we never actually broke up or anything, but since the accident, we've—uh—we've been going our separate ways." He looked at Steven, wondering how he would react to what came next. "But it's not just about Elizabeth. If it were, maybe I wouldn't have a problem. It's also about . . . Jessica."

"Jessica?" Steven repeated, surprised.

"Jessica," Todd confirmed. "We got together a couple times to go to the movies and stuff like that.

She was so torn up about losing Sam, it seemed like she really needed a friend. And I think I thought that being friends with Jessica would lead me back to Elizabeth. Then one night . . ." Todd's face reddened slightly. "Anyway, last night it finally hit me—maybe because it was the first day of the trial—what a mess I've gotten myself into. I've been dating Jessica, but I'm still in love with Elizabeth."

Steven sank back in his chair and stared at Todd, his eyes narrow and unsmiling. "Help me out here, pal. You're telling me that after totally blowing off Liz after the car crash, you're still in love with her, but you've been dating Jessica. Do I have that right?"

Steven's accusatory tone put Todd on the defensive. "She started it," Todd claimed. "She blew *me* off at the prom. She was all over Sam and they *left* together—and even before the prom, for weeks she was acting like a totally different . . ." He broke off, dropping his head in his hands. "I didn't know what to think or what to do, then or now."

"So instead of trying to work things through with Elizabeth, you decided to get back at her by going out with Jessica," Steven summarized, his tone still cool. Pausing to digest it all, he shook his head. "So that's where Jessica's been!"

"I'm not using Jessica to get back at Elizabeth," Todd insisted. "I'm not out for revenge. Look, Jessica called *me*. She made the first move."

"Because she's lonely and scared," said Steven. He took a few swallows of his soda, then placed the can on the coffee table with a bang. "You said it yourself, she needed a friend, and that's probably *all* she needed."

Todd stared down at his hands feeling more guilty and confused than ever. "Do you think I feel good about any of this? Do you think I know which way is up? That's why I came here, to get some advice. And you know, I'm not just thinking about myself—I'm concerned about Liz and Jess, too. But if you don't want to have anything to do with me, I understand."

Todd started to get to his feet. "Hold on," Steven commanded, waving Todd back into his seat. "Just give me a minute, Todd. I need to absorb all this."

For a moment, they sat in silence. Then Steven sighed. "Sorry I came down on you so hard," he said. "I just had no idea what was going on. God, no wonder those two aren't talking to each other."

"So, what do you think I should I do?" Todd asked. "Do you think there's any hope? Do you think Elizabeth would ever take me back?"

"I really don't know," Steven admitted. "You say

you *love* her, but is there any reason she should believe you?"

Steven's words cut like a knife right through Todd's soul.

"Go, Gladiators!" Winston bellowed, cupping his hands around his mouth like a megaphone.

Lila covered her ears. "Geez, Egbert, turn down the volume, would you? They're not even playing—it's halftime!"

Winston checked the clock on the scoreboard. "Well, so it is," he said cheerfully. "Sorry!"

"Maybe you should spend more time watching the game and less time ogling Maria out there cheering," Barry Rork, Amy's boyfriend, ribbed Winston.

The two soccer teams had adjourned to the sidelines for strategy sessions—the game between Sweet Valley High and the Fort Carroll squad was tied. The cheerleaders got to take a break, too. Lila waved to Jessica, Amy, and Maria, who dropped their pom-poms by the home bench and trotted toward the bleachers to join their friends.

"We're tied because you guys aren't yelling loud enough," Amy greeted Lila, Barry, and Winston.

"You *didn't* just hear that," Lila instructed Winston, then turned to Amy. "Don't encourage him!"

"Really, though," said Maria, scanning the skimpy crowd. "It's pretty dead—not much of a turnout today."

"Pamela Robertson from Big Mesa High is here, though," observed Amy.

"You mean, Pamela Robertson from Sweet Valley High," corrected Barry. "She's one of us now."

"One of us?" Jessica sniffed. "Hardly."

Lila twisted in her seat to glance at Pamela, who was sitting alone in the top corner of the bleachers. "Well, at least she's here. Maybe she should get some credit for that."

"I'll give her credit, all right," replied Jessica. "She knows where to go to check out the guys."

"Ouch!" yelped Winston. "That's harsh."

Jessica shrugged carelessly. "It's the truth."

"I don't know." Amy squinted up at Pamela, biting her lip. "I feel a little sorry for her. She looks so lonely. I don't know why she did it, but it took a lot of guts to transfer schools and everybody's avoiding her like the plague."

"Bruce is sure giving her the cold shoulder," commented Barry. "I guess she burned him pretty bad."

"Well, it probably didn't help the situation that *some* people were awfully eager to dish the dirt about her," said Lila with a pointed look at Amy.

86

"Like *you've* never said anything bad about anybody!" Amy protested. Then she sighed. "OK, I'm guilty as charged. I told Bruce what I'd heard through the cheerleader grapevine about Pamela. I guess for some reason—don't ask me why—I just felt like it was my duty to warn him, but now I'm sorry I did it. Are you satisfied?"

"Why should you be sorry?" Jessica asked Amy. "Pamela's a tramp and that's all there is to it."

Lila jumped to Pamela's defense. "Maybe that's not the whole story. Maybe she's really a nice person. How do we know, if we've never even *talked* to her?"

Jessica stared at Lila, her eyebrows raised. "Excuse me, but I think I'm hallucinating. Since when did you join the Girl Scouts?"

The others laughed; Lila smiled wryly without responding. She could hardly believe it herself, but for some reason, she simply had no desire to be cruel and petty even though this was a perfect opportunity. In the past, ridiculing Pamela Robertson would have struck her as a delightful pastime. When she looked up at Pamela's lonely figure, something made her stop. *Maybe I'm getting soft*, she thought to herself with a smile.

"Jessica, hi!" someone called out, interrupting Lila's thoughts.

Lila turned to see Enid making her way toward

them. "Great, it's Florence Nightingale," Jessica muttered under her breath.

"Would you . . . could you give this to Elizabeth for me?" Enid asked hesitantly. She held out a manila folder. "I don't have a car today, so I can't stop by to see her myself. It's just some French homework."

"I suppose so," Jessica said grudgingly, taking the folder with just the tips of her fingers as if it might be contaminated.

Enid mumbled her thanks and scurried off. Lila shook her head. "Boy, that was gracious, Jess!"

"She asked me to do her a favor and I'm doing it—I don't have to be happy about it," Jessica retorted.

"Is Elizabeth managing to keep up with her schoolwork?" Maria asked.

Jessica lifted her shoulders. "How should I know?"

Maria glanced at Amy. "Well, you do live in the same house . . ."

"Well . . . that's all we have in common anymore," Jessica said coldly. "That's all I have in common with anybody in my family, if you ask me. They're all going completely wacko. Elizabeth is walking around like a zombie, my dad's throwing his whole career out the window to defend her, even though they have zero chance of winning, and my mother loses another marble every day. One more," she held up her forefinger for emphasis, "and she won't have any left. I'm just glad Steven's not around enough to realize what's happening." She laughed loudly, gesturing with the folder Enid had given her. "So, that's my family. Not exactly the Cleavers, is it? And you really think that keeping tabs on whether or not my sister is doing her schoolwork is going to remedy the situation?"

Lila and the others stared at Jessica, startled and uncomfortable. At that moment, a whistle indicated the end of the halftime break. Jessica, Amy, and Maria trotted dutifully back to the field.

Stunned, Lila, Barry, and Winston watched them go. It was Winston who finally broke the silence. "I knew Jess was bitter toward Liz, but I've never heard her talk that way about her parents."

It was true, Lila reflected. Lila had always looked at the Wakefields as a model of what a family was supposed to be. Her own family was hardly ideal: her mother had abandoned her when she was a baby, and her father, while giving her everything she could possibly want, had been too busy to give Lila what she really needed.

Now Lila felt a flicker of fear and insecurity. She finally had her own family . . . sort of. *But Mom's only in Sweet Valley temporarily*, Lila reminded herself. *Nothing lasts forever. If I can't count on the stability of the Wakefields, what can I count on?*

"Hey, Bruce, can I come in?" Roger Barrett Patman shouted over the sound of rock music blaring from his cousin's bedroom.

He thought he heard a grunt. Was that a yes? Figuring it was, he pushed Bruce's door open all the way.

Bruce was sitting in front of the personal computer on his desk. He glanced briefly at Roger, then went on typing. When Roger didn't go away, he leaned over with an exaggerated sigh and turned down the volume on his stereo. "All right, you have my full and undivided attention," he said sarcastically. "What's up?"

"Your mom just left to meet your dad in town for dinner," Roger told him. "So you and I are on our own. I thought maybe we could order a pizza or something."

"Fine with me." Bruce reached to turn the stereo back up.

Instead of leaving the room, though, Roger sat down on the edge of Bruce's bed. Bruce raised his eyebrows. "Now what?" he grumbled.

"Actually . . ." Roger pushed his glasses higher on his nose, then cleared his throat. "Actually, I wanted to talk to you about Pamela."

"Pamela." Bruce leaned back in his chair, smiling ironically. "You want to talk to me about Pamela. You did that once before, remember?"

Roger remembered, only too well. He'd been the first person to warn Bruce that he might not know everything there was to know about his new love interest from Big Mesa. He'd been concerned—Bruce had been in a vulnerable emotional state since the death of his girlfriend Regina Morrow. Bruce hid his pain pretty well. He protected himself by making sure he didn't get too close to anybody, and he made sure of *that* by treating the girls he dated like dirt. Then Pamela came along and Bruce fell in love like he was falling off a cliff. Roger just hadn't wanted to see him get hurt.

But he's hurt, all right, Roger thought unhappily, *and so is she, thanks to me.*

"I remember," Roger admitted. "But I never meant for all this to happen."

Bruce folded his arms across his chest. "Spare me."

"Wait, just hear me out," Roger pleaded. "I didn't mean to slam Pamela, or to ruin your relationship. I only wanted to suggest that maybe you should have gone a little slower at first, taken the time to get to know each other before getting so involved. If you had," he added quietly, "maybe you and Pamela would've had a chance."

Roger saw a flicker of emotion in Bruce's eyes. For an instant, Bruce's face softened, the trademark arrogance vanishing.

But just as quickly, the hardness returned. "You weren't the only person who had things to say about Pamela," Bruce told Roger, his bitter tone masking any sadness he might be feeling deep inside.

"At least talk to her," Roger urged. "Let her tell her side of the story. I see her around, and she doesn't seem to have a friend in the world."

Bruce's eyes suddenly blazed with fury. "Who do you think you are? Ann Landers?" he yelled. "Don't you get it by now, Roger? I don't want or need your advice. Live your own life and let me live mine, OK?"

Then Bruce laughed, his attitude shifting abruptly to one of mock insouciance. "Besides, I got what I wanted out of Pamela—the same thing every other guy's gotten from her. I can live with that." Jumping up from his chair, Bruce strode from the room.

Roger heaved a discouraged sigh. This was a repeat of many conversations he'd had with Bruce since he came to live in Sweet Valley after his mother's death. Roger had tried again and again to break through Bruce's shell, but Bruce's pride wouldn't let him. He'd continue to keep his feelings bottled up inside until something triggered another explosion.

As for Pamela, he felt tremendously guilty about exposing her to Bruce, even if he had thought he'd been doing the right thing. At track practice earlier that afternoon, Roger had done lap after lap of the athletic fields. And every time he jogged behind the bleachers, he'd seen her, sitting there at the top, watching the soccer game all by herself.

Getting to his feet, Roger wandered over to Bruce's desk. He peered at the computer screen, half hoping to get some insight into his cousin. Maybe Bruce had been typing Pamela's name over and over. . . .

Nope. There was nothing on the screen but a biology lab report. Roger hit the "save" button so Bruce wouldn't lose his work, then he made a silent vow. *I'll keep an eye out for Pamela—I'll befriend her myself. I think I owe it to her.*

Todd paced the length of his bedroom, still thinking about his visit with Steven. He wished he could outpace his discomfort, but he knew that would be impossible. Steven was right. He'd done terribly by Elizabeth.

So we're all in agreement—I've been a jerk. But

I do love Liz. She might not believe it, but I do. Maybe I could call her, Todd thought hopefully. *I'll apologize, and maybe . . .*

"What, are you nuts?" he said out loud, grabbing a pillow off his bed and pounding it with his fist. "Face it, Wilkins, you missed your chance. It's over. You're *persona non grata* at the Wakefields' these days. Hey." He caught himself with a bitterly ironic laugh. "What am I saying? I've got Jessica!"

Throwing the pillow on the bed, he stalked over to the window. Through the gently waving fronds of a palm tree, he could see the western sky streaked with purple and crimson. Suddenly, Todd's throat tightened with unshed tears as he remembered all the sunsets he'd watched with Elizabeth at his side.

He slapped his hand against the wall. "I can't just give up on her—on us," he declared hoarsely. "Maybe I don't deserve to get her back, but I've got to take a shot at it." He pondered his options. *If I call her, she might just hang up on me. . . . I'll write her a letter!*

Flooded with inspiration, Todd sat down at his desk and grabbed a pen and some paper. He couldn't wait to put his feelings on paper, to tell Elizabeth that he'd been wrong, that their estrangement was all his fault, that he loved her with all his heart, and that her forgiveness was the only thing that could restore his happiness.

But I can't push her, Todd realized, his hand suspended over the blank page. *She'll need time to think things over.*

I'll ask her to give me a sign, he decided after a moment's consideration. He'd go to court every day of her trial—he'd watch and wait patiently. And when Elizabeth wore the silver and turquoise bracelet he'd given her, when she met his eyes and touched the bracelet, he'd know it was OK to go to her.

Yes, Todd thought, his face bright with hopeful conviction, *I'll write it all down and hand-deliver the letter to the house and then I'll wait. I'll wait as long as it takes.*

Chapter 7

I wish this moment could last forever, Lila thought, devouring the scene before her with her eyes, memorizing every detail. *If only . . .*

It was late Thursday afternoon, and she and her parents were having a predinner "cocktail" hour by the swimming pool behind Fowler Crest. *My parents . . . I'm still not used to that,* Lila mused, sipping her cranberry juice and seltzer. *For so long it was just me and Daddy. But this is so much better!*

Lila watched her mother pour herself a glass of white wine and club soda and then squeeze a slice of lime into it. Even such a simple gesture was filled with elegance and beauty. *I guess they knew even when she was a newborn baby,* Lila thought with uncharacteristic sentimentality. *That's why they named her Grace*.

What a relief it was not to be mad at her mother anymore, not to feel so cheated and betrayed about the fact that for sixteen years, her mom had been living halfway around the world in France, and had sought absolutely no contact with her daughter or ex-husband. *I'm glad I've gotten that out of my system*, thought Lila. *What counts is that Mom came to be with me when I needed her. The past doesn't matter—just the present, and the future. . . .*

"You'll never believe where I went today, George, while you were at the office and Lila was in school," Grace said, smiling shyly. She hesitated, as if she weren't sure how he would react to what she was going to say. "That funny little clam bar in Marpa Heights. Remember that old place?"

George Fowler froze in the act of topping a cracker with a wedge of Brie. "Remember?" he exclaimed. "How could I forget? You should have waited for me, though," he added. "We could have driven up there together."

"Well . . ." Grace laughed, waving a perfectly manicured hand. "It wasn't like I was making a *pilgrimage* or anything. I just happened to be driving by."

"What clam bar in Marpa Heights?" Lila piped up. "What's so special about it?"

"Well, Li, if you must know," Mr. Fowler said, winking at Grace, "it was the site of your mother's and my first date."

A clam bar? How unromantic! Lila wrinkled her nose skeptically. "You took mom to a clam bar for your first date?"

Mr. Fowler chuckled. "We were just kids—it seemed like a fine place to me at the time."

"Besides, we'd only just met that very afternoon, about a quarter mile down the beach—it was the closest spot to get a bite to eat," Grace explained. "So maybe it wasn't our first *official* date."

"No, that would've been two nights later," Mr. Fowler agreed, "when we drove down to L.A. to hear jazz at that smoky little club. What was the name of that place?"

Grace tipped her head to one side, her ash-blond hair swinging. "What *was* its name? It was something that sounded like horses. . . ."

Mr. Fowler snapped his fingers. "The Bluegrass Lounge!"

Grace clapped her hands excitedly. "That's it!"

He laughed. "Remember the singer they had that night? That gorgeous woman in the red sequin dress?"

"She walked around all the tables with her microphone and she stopped at ours and sang a song to your father," Grace told Lila, her eyes sparkling.

"She even sat on his lap for a minute. I've never seen anyone's face turn so red!"

Lila was speechless, trying to picture the scene. Her mother and father hanging out at a jazz bar in L.A.? Her parents, "just kids"?

Just kids . . . kids in love.

"We went back a few weeks later," Mr. Fowler recalled.

"A month later," Grace said.

"That's right—it was our one-month anniversary."

"You gave me a dozen red roses," Grace reminisced, "and you asked the band to play—" She broke off, blushing. "Oh, I don't remember the name of the song," she said carelessly.

She's scared, Lila guessed. *She's not sure if Dad wants to remember all of this.*

But he did. He placed his hand lightly, briefly, on Grace's bare arm, his eyes fixed on her face. "You don't? I do. 'It Had to Be You.'"

"Of course," Grace murmured, her eyes shining. "I remember now. That was our song."

Lila's jaw dropped. Now *that* was romantic—roses and jazz and *our* song. . . .

She sat very still and quiet, practically holding her breath. She wanted her parents to forget she was there; she wanted them to go on talking about the days when they were young and falling in love.

Because I don't know anything about it, Lila realized. She'd never thought about what happened *before*: what brought her parents together, what caused them to break up, what made her mother leave her marriage and her child and never look back. For the first time, it occurred to Lila that once there had been something other than distance and estrangement between her parents. Long ago, they'd shared something very special— long ago, they'd been in love.

And now? Lila wondered, studying her parents. Did she see something in their eyes as they looked at each other—a glimmer of interest, a ghost of the old passion?

If it was there, it came and went in a flash. Mr. Fowler cleared his throat; Grace turned away to pour another drink. "Have you had a chance to look up any old friends, Grace?" he asked her in a detached, casual tone.

"I spoke with Dyan Sutton this morning." Grace's expression grew somber. "It wasn't the cheeriest conversation. We talked mostly about Elizabeth Wakefield's trial, and that poor boy who was killed in the car accident. What a terrible tragedy. . . ."

For a moment, the three sat in pensive silence. "It's really horrible," Lila said finally, reaching for a cracker. "The Wakefields are having a really rough time. Supposedly Mrs. Wakefield can't cope at all. I mean, she's like on the *verge*, you know?" Lila shook her head. "She always seemed so together, balancing career and family, and all that stuff. Who'd have expected her to totally come apart at the seams?"

Grace frowned. "Where did you get that story?"

"Straight from the horse's mouth—from Jessica," Lila replied. "She thinks her whole family is going nuts—she's been telling everyone that her dad's acting like a maniac, and her mother's acting like a fruitcake, and she can't relate to her brother at all, and her *sister*—"

"It's very important that the Wakefields all stick together at a time like this," Grace cut in with unexpected vehemence. "Jessica should never forget she only has one family, for better or worse. . . ."

Mrs. Fowler's words trailed off. Lila stared at her mother, startled by the emotion in her voice, confused by the pain in her eyes. *It's almost as if she's not just talking about the Wakefields,* Lila thought. *It's almost as if she's talking about us. . . .*

But Lila was luckier than Jessica. Her own little family had gathered together for the first time in years in a time of trouble, to help her pull through her crisis. And that was a good thing. *So why does Mom look so sad?*

As if reading Lila's mind, Grace stretched out

her hand toward Lila. Lila took it, holding it tight. "What's wrong, Mom?" she asked quietly. "We're all together now, right?"

The desperately hopeful question fell into silence, like a stone sinking to the bottom of a pond. Mr. Fowler stood up to pour himself a drink, turning his back. Grace just squeezed her daughter's hand, wordlessly.

A dissatisfied frown on her face, Jessica flipped through the TV channels with the remote control. Nothing was on, or at least nothing she wanted to watch. Jabbing a button viciously, she switched off the power and tossed the remote aside.

It had been a long, boring Thursday afternoon. All her friends had gone to the beach after school and they'd urged her to join them, but she just hadn't felt like it. Her tan was fading—she'd probably be as pale as Elizabeth soon—but Jessica didn't really care. She didn't care about sunbathing or shopping or any of the things she usually enjoyed.

What's the matter with me? she wondered, rubbing her eyes wearily.

Getting to her feet, she shuffled into the kitchen to get something to eat even though she wasn't really hungry. She found a bowl of guacamole in the refrigerator and tore open a bag of tortilla chips. As she scooped up some guacamole with a chip, she thought about how nice it was to have the house to herself for a change. Both her parents had had to work late because they were taking the next day off to go to court again with Elizabeth; Steven was back on campus, to Jessica's relief; and according to the note she'd left on the kitchen counter, Elizabeth had gone over to Enid's.

Jessica munched a few more chips. Then she made a face. "Ugh, I'm going to get as big as a hippo if I keep eating like this," she said out loud. That wouldn't do at all, especially when Elizabeth was getting thinner by the minute. . . .

Where's that new issue of Sweet Sixteen *that came today?* Jessica wondered, sticking the chips back in the cupboard. *I better get right to that article about how to slim my thighs and tighten my tummy!*

Wandering to the front of the house, she spotted the magazine in a pile of unopened mail on the hall table. She grabbed it and turned to head up the stairs.

As she did, something that looked like an envelope on the floor just inside the front door caught her eye. Jessica walked over and picked it up, her curiosity piqued. It didn't have a stamp—someone must have come by and stuck it through the mail slot themselves. But who?

With a start, Jessica recognized the handwriting on the envelope. Todd's! But the letter wasn't addressed to her. . . . It was for Elizabeth.

Jessica leaned back against the wall and stared blankly at the letter lying in her palm. After a long moment, she laughed out loud, amazed by Todd's stupidity. "Did he really think I wouldn't see this?" she asked the empty hallway.

Then her fingers tightened; she clutched the envelope, wrinkling it. She knew what the letter said as well as if she'd written it herself. She'd seen the lack of enthusiasm in Todd's eyes when they were out together the other night. She'd seen the longing . . . for someone else.

I bet he's begging Elizabeth to take him back. He's ready to throw me aside like an old pair of basketball sneakers. Well, I won't let her take him away from me, Jessica vowed, angrily stuffing the envelope in the back pocket of her jeans. *Not after she stole Sam. She won't get away with it again. And neither will he!*

She should have felt triumphant at the thought of intercepting the letter and foiling Todd's attempts to communicate with Elizabeth. Instead, from out of nowhere a wave of weakness suddenly washed over Jessica, and she felt a stabbing pain in her heart—an unbearable, incurable ache. Incurable because suddenly she understood. She didn't *really* want Todd Wilkins. With all her heart and body and soul, she wanted another boy—a boy she could never see or touch or talk to, never laugh or cuddle with, again. *Never*, ever again.

A flood of hot tears gushed from Jessica's eyes. "Oh, Sam," she sobbed as she slid to the floor, her back against the wall. "Oh, Sam, why did you have to leave me?"

Enid wanted to press her hands against her ears. She couldn't stand to hear Elizabeth recite those words for what seemed like the millionth time. "*I don't remember. . . .*"

Maybe I should have skipped court today, Enid reflected. *It's not like I can do anything for her here. If I'd gone to school instead, I could have given her the notes from the Friday review session in history class, and maybe gotten back that English paper she wrote for Mr. Collins.*

Enid bit her lip. Who was she kidding? Elizabeth *did* need her to be there, and Enid knew it. It was just so painful, having to sit there next to Todd and watch helplessly. Sit and watch Elizabeth stumble through another round of the prosecuting attorney's increasingly impatient questions; watch Ned Wakefield struggle to maintain his professional composure, which threatened to crack at any moment; watch Alice Wakefield look completely detached and undisturbed, somehow removed from the action as if she simply didn't believe it was real, as if she couldn't *bear* for it to be real.

At least the trial is almost over for the day, Enid thought, glancing at her watch. Two days down, and how many more to go? How much longer could this go on?

"Elizabeth," Mr. Dilworth said, standing in front of Elizabeth and forcing her to meet his eyes. "What were you wearing the night of the prom?"

"A . . . a blue dress," Elizabeth answered, seeming puzzled by the question.

"What kind of flowers were in your corsage?"

"They were . . ." Elizabeth darted a quick glance in Todd's direction. "White roses."

"Did you wear any perfume, any jewelry?"

Elizabeth described the jewelry she'd worn. "No perfume, though," she told the prosecutor.

"Hmm." Mr. Dilworth folded his arms across his chest. "You have a pretty good recollection of those details," he observed.

"It—it was a big night."

"It *was* a big night," he agreed. "So, tell me." He waved an arm out at the audience. "Tell us all. Why do you remember some things perfectly, but other things not at all. Is it possible, Elizabeth," he boomed, pointing an accusing finger at her, "is it *possible* you don't remember certain things because you don't *want* to remember them? Because you can't bring yourself to confront your own guilt in the death of Sam Woodruff?"

All around the courtroom, there were murmurs and exclamations. "How dare he?" Enid gasped. "How *dare* he?" And why didn't Mr. Wakefield protest? Why didn't he fight back? Enid stared at Elizabeth's father, waiting for him to jump up and cry, "Objection!" It didn't happen. Ned Wakefield ran a hand over his face, his eyes on the yellow legal pad that lay on the table in front of him. *Has he given up?* Enid wondered. Was he, too, conceding that this was an open-and-shut case, that his own daughter was guilty?

Enid looked back at Elizabeth. Even from a distance, she could see the tears brim in her best friend's eyes. But Elizabeth didn't break down. "I . . . don't . . . remember," she repeated with desperate certainty. "Maybe you don't believe me, but it's true."

The prosecutor stared hard at her for a long moment. "No further questions," he said at last.

"You may step down," Judge Baird told Elizabeth. Then she struck her gavel and declared, "Court is adjourned until Monday morning."

The members of the audience rose to their feet, their voices rising with them. Enid stood on her tiptoes, trying to see Elizabeth. Together, she and Todd pushed toward the aisle.

Flanked by her parents, Elizabeth began walking past them, out of the courtroom. Her pace was slow and measured; she stared straight ahead with wide, unseeing eyes.

"Liz," Enid said softly, stepping forward and stretching out her hand.

Elizabeth turned her head slightly. She didn't look at Enid, however; she looked at Todd.

Beside her, Enid felt Todd stiffen. An intense, hopeful light leapt into his eyes. He seemed to be holding his breath, to be searching for something in Elizabeth's face, waiting for a word or gesture.

It didn't come. Elizabeth didn't speak; she didn't even blink. Her eyes were like the eyes painted on the face of a china doll, blank and blind. *She doesn't really see him,* Enid realized. *She doesn't see any of us.*

Elizabeth passed on, leaving Todd staring after her, his expression tortured and hopeless. "C'mon, Todd," Enid said softly. She slipped her arms into the sleeves of her jacket. "Let's go."

As they started into the aisle, Enid turned to look back toward the judge's bench. *Mr. Wakefield said the trial would probably only take three days,* Enid reflected. *That means on Monday, it may be all over.* She shuddered involuntarily as she pictured the scene, imagining the moment when the judge rendered her decision. *"I find the defendant . . .*

guilty." What if that's her verdict?

Enid shook her head, bringing herself back to the present moment. She refocused on the figure of the bailiff, who'd remained after the judge retired to her chambers. The bailiff was talking to a nervous-looking young man wearing a baseball cap and a college sweatshirt. Enid didn't recognize him, and she didn't even have the mental energy to wonder who he was.

All she could think about was Monday, and her fear of what was going to happen to her best friend. The evidence was just too incontrovertible. In the end, did it really matter whether Elizabeth remembered anything or not? *She* had been *drunk and she* had been *driving,* Enid thought, feeling more hopeless than she ever had in her entire life. *Oh, Elizabeth, what's going to become of you?*

Chapter 8

Steven strode across the main quadrangle on Friday afternoon, a grouchy expression on his face. He wasn't sure what he was more annoyed about: the fact that he hadn't been able to attend Elizabeth's trial that day because of an economics exam he couldn't reschedule, or the probability that he'd failed the exam regardless because he'd been too distracted to study.

A voice broke into his dismal reverie. "Hey, Wakefield!" someone called.

Steven looked up, narrowing his eyes against the bright sun. When he saw who was hurrying toward him, his annoyance increased. Bart Lloyd had been a year ahead of him at Sweet Valley High, and this semester they had a political science class together. Bart tended to be a pompous jerk; he wasn't Steven's favorite person in the best of times, and today Steven really didn't think he could stand to exchange even a few words with him. *Plus, he probably just wants to borrow my poli-sci notes,* Steven thought cynically.

"Hi," Steven said briskly.

He planned to blow right past Bart, but Bart stepped in front of him and put a hand on his arm, giving Steven no choice but to put on the brakes.

"Wakefield, just wanted to tell you I'm sorry about your sister," Bart said with an irritating mixture of condescension and curiosity.

Steven really didn't want to talk about Elizabeth with Bart. "Thanks," he muttered, shrugging off the other boy's hand. "She's doing OK. See ya around."

But Bart wasn't finished. "And I'm sorry about your mom, too," he continued.

"My mom?" Steven repeated.

"Yeah. I heard she's really gone over the edge over this—really lost her marbles. Isn't she in the hospital or something?"

Steven's jaw dropped. Then he clenched his teeth shut, his face red with anger and embarrassment. "No, she's not in the hospital," he snapped. "And she *didn't* go over the edge."

Bart lifted his shoulders. "Sorry, man. That's just the story I heard."

"Well, it's a lie," Steven declared, his voice rising. "Whoever told you, told you wrong."

"OK, OK. Sorry," Bart repeated. "If I hear anybody else talking, I'll set them straight."

He gave Steven a friendly slap on the shoulder. "So long, Wakefield," he said, sauntering off across the lawn.

Steven stared after Bart, breathing hard. *"That's just the story I heard. . . ."* *Who would say a thing like that?* Steven wondered. *Who would spread such a cruel rumor?*

He had to admit to himself, the worst part was that the exaggerated story had a grain of truth to it. He raked a hand through his hair. *But outside of the family, no one knows about Mom,* he thought, baffled. *No one else knows how bad she really is . . . right?*

"Don't forget the party tonight at Barry's," Amy called to Jessica as they parted after cheerleading practice Friday afternoon. "You'd better be there!"

"I will be," Jessica lied with false cheerfulness. "See ya."

Her friends headed for the women's locker room. Jessica left the fitness room through another door that opened into the main gymnasium.

She saw quickly that her hunch had been correct. Todd had been absent from school that day—he'd gone to the trial, obviously—but he'd gotten out in time for basketball practice.

Jessica took a seat in the bleachers, picking a spot where she had a good view of Todd . . . and he had an equally good view of her. He noticed her in the middle of a drill that involved pivoting around a defensive guard at midcourt and then shooting. He glimpsed her out of the corner of his eye just as the basketball left his fingertips; as it swished through the net, he did a double take.

With my hair in a ponytail I look even more like Elizabeth, Jessica thought sourly. She flashed Todd a sugar-sweet smile, though, and gave him a perky wave. Todd jerked his chin up, acknowledging her . . . just barely.

For half an hour, Jessica watched Todd sweat out every drill as if he were trying out for the Olympics. Part of her looked on in a detached, objective fashion—she appreciated his speed and skill as she would any other talented athlete's. Sure, he was good-looking, but so were some of the other guys on the team. Another part of her, though, looked at Todd with a need, a hunger, that grew more urgent with every passing minute. She wanted to run her fingers through his damp hair; she wanted to pull him close, to crush herself

114

against his broad chest. She needed Todd—she needed his strength. Without it, Jessica knew that she simply might not have the will to go on acting out her life.

And if I don't keep pressing, she thought desperately, *he's going to slip through my fingers. He'll go crawling back to her. . . .*

A whistle blew and Todd and his teammates jogged over to the sidelines to hear the coach's wrap-up. Practice was over.

Jessica got to her feet. As the rest of the team streamed toward the locker room, Todd grabbed a towel and headed back in her direction.

"Great practice," Jessica greeted him.

Todd gave her a halfhearted smile. "I only shot sixty percent from the foul line," he said. "Pretty lame."

"Still, you deserve a reward," she said playfully. "How about a sunset picnic at the beach? I know a cove down at Moon Beach where nobody ever goes. . . ."

Todd shook his head. "I don't think so, Jess," he mumbled into the towel as he wiped his forehead.

"We could go to a movie if you'd rather," she offered. "Get a pizza first, of course. I'm ravenous, aren't you?"

"No . . . not really."

He glanced over his shoulder, clearly poised for

flight. *You don't have to be a genius to read* his *body language,* Jessica thought, tears of anger and frustration jumping into her eyes.

"Fine," she said, trying to sound casual, ready to flounce out of the gym. "If you're so busy—"

"Jess, wait." Todd grabbed her arm. He looked down at her tear-streaked face, a mix of emotions battling in his dark eyes. Compassion won out. "It's just . . . not tonight. Tomorrow, maybe."

"OK," Jessica said, mollified. "Tomorrow."

He squeezed her arm and then let his hand drop back to his side. But instead of leaving he lingered, gazing intently at her, as if there were something else he wanted to say.

Jessica stepped closer to him, her spirits lifting. *He* does *want to go out with me,* she thought. *He's coming to his senses—he's realizing he'd be crazy to blow me off.*

Then, in a flash of intuition, Jessica guessed the truth. He wasn't even thinking about her. *The letter. He wants to know if Elizabeth got his letter. He's trying to come up with a way to find out without actually asking me outright.*

Jessica's heart contracted with a knifelike pain. She wanted to slap Todd across the face with all her might—she wanted to hurt him back. But she resisted the urge.

"You know, Todd," she said, her voice steady, "if

116

you're worried about Liz, you shouldn't be. She doesn't deserve your sympathy—she doesn't need it. She doesn't need *any* of us. She won't take phone calls anymore, even from Enid." Jessica didn't even hesitate over this lie. It sounded right—it fit the picture she wanted to paint of Elizabeth as a lost cause, completely unredeemable. "And yesterday . . . yesterday she got a letter from someone, I don't know who."

Todd's eyes lit up with hopeful expectation. "Well, she read it," Jessica continued, shaking her head sadly, "and then she ripped it up and threw it away. You wouldn't know her anymore, Todd. She's like a rock these days—cold and hard."

She watched with satisfaction as the light faded from Todd's eyes. "She's like a rock," Jessica repeated, gently but firmly tapping the last nail into the coffin of Todd and Elizabeth's love. "It doesn't look like anyone's ever going to get through to her again."

Bruce double-faulted for the second time in a row, throwing yet another game to Chad. "Get your act together, Patman," he grumbled to himself as he and Chad switched sides on the tennis court. Usually he made short work of Chad when they were paired up during practice—after all, he was the team's top seed and Chad was only seeded eighth. But this afternoon, for some reason, he simply couldn't keep his mind on the game or his eye on the ball.

For some reason . . . Bruce knew what the reason was, only too well. Just a few courts away, the girls' tennis team was holding practice. And today, somebody new was trying out for the team.

Out of the corner of his eye, Bruce watched Pamela run for a backhand. She returned it, low and hard. Wendy Gibson lobbed it back to her, and Pamela put it away with an overhead smash that would have done credit to a Wimbledon winner.

Meanwhile, Chad served, acing Bruce on his first try. Chad raised his eyebrows, surprised. "Hey, I didn't know I was that good!" he called out cheerfully.

"Yeah, well, you're not," Bruce muttered under his breath.

Chad served again and Bruce slammed a monster forehand, pushing Chad way back past the baseline. Chad's return went into the net. "Hmph," Bruce grunted with satisfaction. *Take that, you squirt.*

He couldn't maintain his concentration, though. Chad matched him, point for point. The game went to deuce. Bruce had the advantage, but lost it. It was advantage Ticknor—game point for Chad—which meant Bruce couldn't afford to be distracted even for a millisecond. But he was the pawn of emotional forces beyond his control; he couldn't help being more aware of Pamela, two courts away, than he was of his own opponent right across the net.

She's better than any of the girls already on the team, he observed, feeling an absurd, inappropriate rush of pride. On the tennis court, Pamela really had it all: skill, power, and strategy. And her every move was suffused with beauty and grace—she was poetry in motion.

Bruce remembered the day he tracked Pamela down at Big Mesa High. He'd found her practicing with the tennis team, and even though he'd never really talked to her, he'd fallen in love just watching her play. Then and there, he'd known she was the one.

Bruce fought back to deuce, regaining the advantage. *So, you "knew," eh?* he said to himself. *You didn't know diddly.*

He swung recklessly at the ball, missing an easy shot. He tried to focus on Chad's next serve, but it was impossible when his thoughts were a whirl of longing, confusion, and anger, spinning as fast as the tennis ball. *How could she appear to be one thing,* Bruce wondered, *as sweet and beautiful as an angel, and turn out to be the exact opposite?* He took a sloppy swing, swatting the ball into the net.

119

And if I'm through with her, why can't I stop thinking about her?

"Advantage Ticknor," Chad announced.

Bruce gritted his teeth. *All right, enough of this fooling around,* he lectured himself. *Let's get serious.*

Chad tossed the ball in the air and smashed it across the net at Bruce. Bruce returned the serve, then rushed to the net. He was ready for Chad's next shot, and when it came, he slammed it into the corner of the court for the point. Back in command, Bruce won the next point, and the game, and the set.

Practice over, he zipped his racket into its case, meanwhile stealing a glance at Pamela at the other end of the courts. The girls were done with practice, too, and she was helping the rest of the team gather up loose tennis balls. Quickly, Bruce calculated the odds that he'd bump into her on his way in or out of the gym. *I'll skip the locker room today,* he decided. *I can shower at home.*

Grabbing his warm-up jacket, Bruce headed down the sidewalk toward the student parking lot. He reached one corner of the lot at the same moment that a slender, dark-haired girl in a tennis dress entered at another corner, having taken a shortcut from the courts through a grove of trees.

Bruce caught his breath. Was Pamela thinking

along the same lines he was and hurrying to the parking lot in order to avoid him? Or was she trying to intercept him? He supposed the motive didn't matter. He realized her car was parked just a few spaces away from his Porsche—they were on a collision course.

When she recognized Bruce, Pamela checked her stride momentarily. As they drew nearer to each other, he could see that her face was turning bright pink. She certainly didn't *look* as if she'd been expecting to run into him.

A few more steps, and they were face-to-face. Bruce had to pass Pamela to get to his car; she had to pass him to get to *her* car. Bruce bowed in an ironic fashion, ushering her by with a sweeping gesture. "After you," he said snidely.

Their eyes met and Pamela's blush deepened. She opened her mouth as if to say something, then snapped it shut and hurried on toward her car.

Bruce turned on his heel, staring after her. He was almost disappointed that she hadn't talked back to him. *Who could blame her, though, when I've been acting so obnoxious?* he thought with a twinge of guilt.

Why was that, anyway? When Pamela was so clearly shy and vulnerable around him, why did he feel compelled to hurt her? Was it because he knew otherwise it would be too easy to relent, to meet her halfway?

Clenching his teeth, Bruce fought down his guilt—and his secret, pathetic, wimpy, inexcusable desire to make up with her. *She's not the injured one*, he reminded himself. *You're wasting your time feeling sorry for her—she's not as sweet and helpless as she looks.*

"Heading home already, Pamela?" he heard himself call after her. "Why not stick around school a little longer? You could catch the tail end of football practice, or do you like basketball players better?" Pamela turned back toward him, her eyes stricken. For some reason, her pain only egged Bruce on. "No, let me guess," he drawled. "You'd rather sit in on a faculty meeting—you're ready for some older men."

Laughing at his own wit, Bruce climbed into the Porsche and started the engine. He didn't give Pamela another glance—that was part of her punishment—but as he backed out of the parking space, he couldn't help glimpsing her in the side mirror. In the instant before he roared off, leaving her standing in a cloud of dust, he could see the tears streaming down her face.

Billie was sitting at the kitchen table doing homework when Steven stormed into the apartment on Friday evening. He slammed the door behind him; he was furious and he didn't care who knew it. In fact, he *wanted* Billie to know it—he fully intended that she should hear all about it. Because he was furious with *her*.

She glanced up at him, raising her eyebrows. "What's wrong?" she asked, a worried note in her voice.

Steven smiled humorlessly. "I'll tell you what's wrong," he replied. "I bumped into Bart Lloyd a while ago, and do you know what he said?"

Billie shook her head. "Why don't you sit down and tell me?" she suggested, patting the chair next to her.

Steven walked over to the table and yanked out another chair directly across from her. He dropped into it, glaring at Billie. "Bart asked me how my mother was doing," he began in a barely controlled voice. "According to him, everyone on campus is talking about how she's cracked up completely. Now where do you think he could have gotten a story like that?"

Steven didn't even try to keep the note of accusation out of his tone. Billie stared at him, confused. Then it registered. Her eyes widened, and she reached out, touching Steven's hand. "Steven, you don't think *I* told him?"

Steven snatched his hand away. "That's exactly what I *do* think," he declared, his voice hoarse. The pain and anger surged up in him as he relived the moment when he'd figured it out. After his encounter with Bart, he'd puzzled over who might have revealed Mrs. Wakefield's problems, and suddenly he'd remembered one person outside of the family who knew—Billie. Just as suddenly, it had dawned on him that he knew next to nothing about his new roommate. He'd trusted her with all his secrets, leaned on her during this trying time . . . and, yes, allowed himself to develop a crush on her. What a mistake!

She couldn't care less about me, Steven thought, his throat tightening with tears. *She was just pretending, just using me, buttering me up because she had a good thing living here. Why on earth did I trust her?*

"You told Bart or someone else. What does it matter now?" Steven felt his face about to crumple, but he willed himself to hold on to his self-control. He would *not* cry in front of her. "You betrayed me."

Billie shook her head slowly. "No, Steven," she whispered, her own eyes bright with tears. "It's *you* who've betrayed *me.*"

Steven didn't respond. He didn't have the strength to argue with her, and he didn't trust himself—he was afraid that if he opened his mouth again, he might scream or, worse, sob.

I just wish she would go away, he thought hopelessly.

As if she'd read his mind, Billie rose to her feet. "OK," she said quietly. "I'm sorry. I'll leave in the morning."

Steven looked up quickly, all at once feeling panicked. Maybe he didn't want her to go away; maybe he didn't want to be left alone. "Wait . . ." he began.

But Billie had made up her mind. Setting her lips in a firm line, she turned on her heel and marched to her bedroom, shutting the door behind her with a bang.

The sound pierced Steven's heart like a bullet. A wave of loneliness and desolation washed over him and he slumped in his chair, the strength draining from his body. He felt like a drowning man sinking into deep water, his life ring having just slipped from his fingers. "Oh, Billie," Steven whispered, dropping his head heavily onto his folded arms.

Chapter 9

Elizabeth stepped off the bus at a stop just a few blocks from the Sweet Valley town beach. It felt a little funny, taking public transportation, but these days, with her driver's license suspended indefinitely, the bus was her only option.

Still, she would have walked if she'd had to. As she neared the grassy dunes, Elizabeth paused to take a deep breath of the fresh, salty air. She felt better instantly, just the way she knew she would. She felt cleansed.

It was a Sunday afternoon and the beach was fairly crowded, so she headed up the shore, away from the volleyball games, the children building sand castles, the picnickers, the wave riders. She walked briskly, her feet digging deeply into the soft, sun-warmed sand. *I could walk forever,* Elizabeth thought dreamily, her eyes on the distant cliffs. Suddenly, something occurred to her. *I could walk forever—literally. I could just leave. I could run away from home—run away from everything!*

With an odd, rueful smile, Elizabeth sat down on a piece of driftwood facing the ocean. She knew she wouldn't do it. As crazy and horrible as her world had become, as miserable and confused as she was, she could never run away. She had to take responsibility for her actions—she had to face the music. Wasn't that what suffering through the trial was all about?

Besides, I couldn't really *run away,* Elizabeth thought, tossing a pebble into the waves. *I couldn't run away from* myself. *I'd still be me. I'd carry what I did, what I did to Sam, with me wherever I went.*

For a long time she sat, motionless and quiet, watching the waves roll in. It was incredibly soothing, almost hypnotic. A wave would crash in a shower of white foam and then it would be sucked back into the sea—to be followed by another and another and another, endlessly. . . .

The ocean never changes. It never ends, Elizabeth reflected. Suddenly, she was reminded of a night not too long ago—the night a gang of kids from Big Mesa High raided a Sweet Valley High beach party. It had been a pivotal occasion in more ways than one: the beginning of a heated rivalry between Sweet Valley and Big Mesa, and the start of new tensions between Elizabeth and Jessica, too. At one point during the party, Bruce had dared Jessica to swim out to a buoy and back again, in the dark. Elizabeth had begged Jessica not to do it, afraid that Jessica would swim out into the night and never return.

Now Elizabeth found herself wondering how Jessica had felt as she stroked blindly through the dark, cold water. Was she scared, or just exhilarated?

Standing up, Elizabeth kicked off her sneakers and walked toward the water. She waded in, up to her calves, up to her knees. *What would it be like?* she wondered, curious. *What's out there? What is it like, Sam?*

Tears sprang to Elizabeth's eyes. She shook her head, hard. "I'm the lucky one," she choked out. "No matter what I'm going through, no matter what's in store for me after tomorrow, I'm the lucky one. I'm *alive*."

Elizabeth turned and walked out of the sea. Retrieving her shoes, she headed back down the shore toward the parking lot and the bus stop . . . and home.

Jessica turned up the volume on her stereo Sunday night, blasting the music in an attempt to drown out the noise in her brain. It didn't work. She couldn't stop thinking about what was going on downstairs.

With a disgruntled sigh, she switched the stereo off altogether. *Maybe I'll just go down and take a quick peek*, she decided. She'd satisfy her curiosity, and then she could forget about Elizabeth and the trial. It really was of no concern to her, after all.

On soundless bare feet, Jessica padded down the hall to the staircase. Already, she could hear the voices.

She could hear the voices . . . and the stress, the frustration, the fear. *Dad and Steven are trying one last time to get some information from Liz,* Jessica guessed. *And it's still not working.*

She sat down on the bottom step in the shadowy front hallway, where she could see the scene in the living room without being noticed herself. Elizabeth was sitting on the couch next to Steven, a blank, surreal expression on her face. Mr. Wakefield stood in front of her, a pencil behind his ear and a legal pad in his hand. And Mrs. Wakefield . . .

What is she doing? Jessica wondered, watching as her mother spritzed window cleaner on one of the front windowpanes, then energetically rubbed it dry with a paper towel. *Geez, of all times to be washing windows!*

"This is what I've put together for tomorrow so far," Mr. Wakefield said to Elizabeth, holding up the legal pad.

Even Jessica could see that the pad was blank. Steven winced; Elizabeth didn't even blink.

"Only *you* can put words on this paper," Mr. Wakefield told his daughter with unaccustomed sternness. "More than anything in the world, Liz, I want to help you, but in order to do that, *you* have to help *me*." His voice softened. "This is our last chance, honey. Most likely, the trial will wrap up tomorrow. This is our last chance to be heard. So, tell me," he urged. "Tell me what happened the night of the accident."

"I can't tell you what I don't know," Elizabeth said in a voice devoid of all emotion. Her gaze shifted; she was watching Mrs. Wakefield whisk around the room with a feather duster. "Don't you think I would, if I could?"

Mrs. Wakefield breezed past Jessica on her way into the kitchen. She reappeared a moment later with a tray of drinks and snacks. Jessica followed her mother as far as the entrance to the liv-

131

ing room and stood watching her family from there.

It was a bizarre and disturbing tableau. Her father and Elizabeth remained locked in a hopeless stalemate; her mother's unnatural happy-homemaker behavior only fueled the tension, like a log on a fire. With a bright smile, Mrs. Wakefield offered the tray. Mr. Wakefield waved it away, his expression testy; Steven's face clouded with concern. And Elizabeth just sat motionless and composed, as if she knew the worst was inevitable but was resigned to it.

Jessica stood rooted to the spot, mesmerized. *Tomorrow is the day*, she thought. *The third and final day. Elizabeth is going to be found guilty of manslaughter.*

All at once, an odd sensation rushed over Jessica. It was as if she were swept out of her body, and suddenly looking down from above at the scene . . . and at herself.

How can I be so calm? she asked herself desperately. *How can I stand this?*

She clenched her hands into tight fists; if she didn't, she was afraid she might start shaking. She might start shaking—crying—screaming. She might just fly apart into a million pieces. Her heart was ready to burst; her secret was struggling to get out. Her horrible secret . . .

"Jessica."

Jessica jumped. "What?" she cried, startled, guilty.

It was her father who had spoken. He was looking at her; they were all looking at her.

"Jessica, come here," he pleaded, his voice low and urgent. "Join us. Please."

Jessica stared at her parents and Steven and Elizabeth, warring impulses raging within her. She was torn between wanting to run to her family and wanting to run away from them . . . and away from herself and the awful truth of how Elizabeth came to be drunk and why she had driven off the road the night of the Jungle Prom. The awful truth of who was *really* responsible for Sam's death.

Jessica didn't respond to her father's request. Biting back the words of self-condemnation that welled up from deep inside her, she turned and fled from the room.

As Margo stepped off the bus on Sunday evening, her eyes lit up, shining as brightly as the neon signs that flickered all around her. *I'm here,* she thought reverently. *The City of Angels. Los Angeles, California. I'm here!*

She wanted to jump, to sing, to dance. After so many long, dusty days, after countless hours and endless miles, she'd come to the end of the line.

The bus stopped here, and it didn't go any farther.

But I'm not quite *to the end of* my *road*, Margo reminded herself. Shouldering her bag, she strode purposefully into the crowded transportation terminal and looked around for the appropriate sign. There it was: NORTHBOUND TRAINS—TICKET SALES.

Margo crossed to the counter. "I'd like to buy a ticket to Sweet Valley," she informed the clerk.

"One way or round trip?" he inquired.

For the first time in ages, a smile of genuine pleasure illuminated Margo's face. "One way," she replied.

Five minutes later, she was back on the sidewalk, the precious ticket tucked safely in the pocket of the shorts she'd just changed into in the women's room. And now she was hungry. She looked around for a place to eat, her mouth watering at the thought of a real meal, hot and home-cooked. *I'm going to treat myself*, she decided as she walked toward a diner on the corner. *I'm going to celebrate.*

A few people glanced up at her as she entered the diner and made her way to the counter—a few *men*. Margo smiled to herself as she sat down on a stool and crossed her legs seductively. She knew she looked good, and she *felt* good—better than she'd ever felt in her life. Because for the first time in her life, everything was going her way; she was doing everything right. She'd figured out how to overcome the obstacles that stood in her path, how to deal with the people who tried to keep her down. She used to be a pawn of forces beyond her control; now she was smart and beautiful and powerful. She was in charge.

And this is only the beginning, Margo thought. The world had only just opened up to her—she was only just reaching out to take what was rightfully hers. As soon as she got to Sweet Valley, she'd grab it—she'd grab it all.

With a sigh of satisfaction, Margo tossed back her glossy dark hair and reached for a menu. A waitress stood ready to take her order, pen and notepad in hand. "Let's see," Margo murmured, drawing out the pleasure of choosing. "I think I'll have . . . the California burger."

"Fries or coleslaw with that?" the waitress asked briskly.

"Fries. And a large iced tea, please."

Margo stuck the menu back in between the ketchup bottle and the saltshaker. She rested her elbow on the table, cupping her chin in her hand, and swung her bare leg gently. She knew she made a pretty picture, and gradually she became aware that someone was watching her.

Out of the corner of her eye, she could tell that he was young and tall and fair-haired. *A California boy,* she thought, suppressing a smirk. *They're the same out here as they are everywhere.* If she really set her mind to it, how long would it take her? Thirty seconds? A minute? How long before she could lure him to her and have him wrapped around her finger, ready to do her every bidding?

It's getting way too easy, she thought, sipping the iced tea the waitress had placed in front of her. Drop a few well-chosen words, show a little leg . . . where was the challenge anymore?

The man continued to watch her. After a few minutes, Margo grew uneasy. He wasn't just admiring her; there was something aggressive and relentless about his gaze. It began to madden her—and frighten her. It diminished that precious new feeling of absolute self-command she'd been savoring just a moment before.

Margo knew how to fix him. She had made him look—now she'd make him look away. Slowly, she turned her head, ready to freeze the man with an icy, discouraging glare.

Instead, she was the one who froze. Her eyes widened like those of a deer caught in the headlights of an oncoming car, and her heart leapt into her throat, nearly choking her. It wasn't a stranger who'd been staring at her. It was Josh Smith, Georgie's older brother!

Quickly, Margo faced forward again. Her head spun; for an instant, she felt as if she might faint. *How did he find me?* she wondered, breathing fast. *Has he been following me all the way from Ohio? How am I going to get away from him?*

She sensed her power slipping away from her. She knew she could fall apart just like that. *But I won't. I won't do it,* she determined. *I won't lose what I've fought so hard for.*

She took a deep breath, forcing herself to calm down and stay in control. *See what happens when you let your guard down?* she said sharply to herself. *Never, ever let your guard down.*

Out of the corner of her eye, she saw Josh stand up and begin to walk toward her with slow, purposeful strides. She steeled herself for the encounter. *He has no proof,* she reminded herself. *Absolutely no proof that I had anything to do with Georgie's death, or the robbery.* She was in a tight spot, but she'd been in tight spots before. She'd get out of this one the way she had all the others. *I have nothing to be afraid of. . . .*

The waitress had just brought Margo's food. Margo kept her eyes on her plate as Josh sat down on the next stool. He leaned closer to her, until she could smell him. He smelled like soap and sweat.

He smelled like danger . . . but, she thought triumphantly to herself, he also smelled like fear.

"Don't bother trying to run," Josh said to her, his voice low so that only she could hear. "Your running days are over."

"Pardon me?" Margo said loudly. "I don't believe I know you. I've never seen you before."

It worked; a few people turned to look in their direction. Josh shifted uncomfortably on his stool. "I'm onto you," he continued with a bit less confidence. "I know about the fire in New York, and the death of the little girl. And I know you're the one responsible for Georgie's death." His voice cracked. "I'm onto you," he repeated, louder now. "And in about one minute, I'm going to turn you over to the police."

Margo kept her expression blank, not revealing a thing. She knew she could win this face-off, if she held her cards close to her chest while Josh scattered his all over the table. Didn't he know he was making the fatal mistake? Didn't he know you had to keep your emotions in check if you wanted to get your way? Didn't he know that cool, calm control would always triumph over passion and heat?

"I wanted to see you again before you're locked up, though," Josh told Margo. "Locked up for good, as you should be. You're a sick girl, Michelle, or whatever your name is." His voice shook with fury and pain and disgust. He jumped to his feet, grabbing her arm. "A sick—"

"What do you think you're doing?" Margo shouted, her voice high-pitched with outrage and distress. "Get your hands off me! I told you, I've never seen you before in my life!"

The sudden outburst threw Josh off balance. Instantly, a number of people hurried to Margo's aid. "Hey, buddy, what's going on?" one man demanded, seizing Josh's arm and pulling him away from Margo.

"What do you think you're doing, giving the lady a hard time?" asked another man.

Suddenly, the whole diner was in chaos. Somebody jostled a waitress; she dropped a plate and it shattered all over the floor. Josh raised his voice above the din, trying to explain. "She's lying!" he yelled. "She *does* know me—she murdered my brother! I'm telling you, she's wanted by the police! Don't let her get away!"

But it was too late. Margo saw her opportunity and took it without hesitation. As Josh was restrained by the men who'd jumped to defend her, Margo gave them all the slip, ducking out of the diner.

She took a rapid, circuitous route back to the train station, walking fast rather than running. She couldn't risk drawing attention to herself. Now more than ever, anonymity was her only hope.

At the entrance to the station, she glanced over her shoulder. She didn't see Josh, or any police officers. But that didn't mean they wouldn't come after her.

She couldn't risk it—she couldn't risk anyone following her to Sweet Valley.

Margo hastened to the ticket counter. "Excuse me, but could I possibly exchange this ticket?" she asked, handing over her ticket to Sweet Valley. "I'd like to go to . . ." She needed a town in the opposite direction. ". . . San Diego instead."

"Here you go," the clerk said, giving her a new ticket. "But you'd better hurry—the San Diego train's about to leave. Track nine!" he called after Margo, who'd already started to run toward the platform.

She jumped on board just as the southbound train started to move. Careening down the aisle, she sank, weak-kneed and breathless, into the first empty seat.

She leaned back against the old vinyl, her eyes closed and her entire body rigid from the adrenaline that was pumping through it. *That was a close call,* Margo thought, shivering as she remembered the moment she'd recognized Josh. Had she shaken him? Her whole life depended on it. She was so close to her dream now—she

140

couldn't let anything happen to destroy it. . . .

"Your ticket, ma'am. Ma'am, your ticket, please."

Distracted, Margo didn't hear the conductor until he'd asked for her ticket three times. "Oh, sorry," she mumbled, giving him the sweaty and crumpled ticket she'd been clutching in her fingers.

The train rumbled out of the station. Through the window, Margo saw the L.A. skyline. Five minutes passed, then ten, and she remained undisturbed. No one approached her—no one had followed her onto the train.

Suddenly, Margo smiled. She'd had a brush with exposure—Josh had almost cornered her—but she'd turned the tables. She'd come out ahead. She was still free. He thought he was so smart, tracking her down like that. But *she* was the clever one!

Margo let out a loud, unbidden laugh. Several people sitting nearby turned to stare at her, their eyes suspicious.

Slumping in her seat, Margo hid her smile behind the pages of a magazine she pulled from her shoulder bag. She couldn't give herself away now, not when she was so close. She had to learn from Josh's mistake. She had to be extremely careful to suppress her emotions and watch her every step.

All will come in due time, Margo reminded herself, her eyes glittering with anticipation. *In due time, I'll be happy. I'll have everything I've ever wanted,* be *everything I've ever wanted to be. In due time . . . but not before.*

Chapter 10

"Dilworth and I have been called to the judge's chambers," Ned Wakefield said to Steven as they stood in the lobby of the courthouse on Monday morning. "I'll see you inside."

"What's it about?" Steven asked.

"I don't know, son." Mr. Wakefield's tone was gloomy; clearly, he didn't look upon the summons as good news. "We'll find out soon enough." He gave Steven's arm a brief squeeze. "Take care of your mother."

"I will," Steven promised.

He watched his father until Mr. Wakefield disappeared down the long corridor. Then Steven took a deep breath and squared his shoulders, trying to prepare himself mentally for the grueling morning that lay ahead of them. *This is it,* Steven thought grimly, adjusting the knot in his necktie. He'd worn his best suit because he knew that, one way or another, he'd probably get his picture in the newspaper. Today was the day.

He glanced at his mother, who was standing in a corner of the lobby with Jessica. Steven was glad to see that having Jessica with her seemed to steady Mrs. Wakefield somewhat. Jessica . . . Steven shook his head. She was a puzzler. He didn't quite understand why she'd decided to make this eleventh-hour appearance at the trial; it certainly didn't represent a change of heart, as she still wasn't speaking to Elizabeth. Elizabeth, meanwhile, was already seated inside the courtroom, shielded from the crush of reporters and spectators.

Tense and anxious, Steven paced up and down, waiting for the signal that the morning session was about to commence. He wanted to feel positive. He knew everyone was looking at him and, for the sake of his family, he tried to exude optimism and confidence. But he had a feeling he wasn't pulling it off. The dread he felt inside just had to be visible on his face; he simply didn't have the strength to hide it anymore.

Steven stuck his hands deep in his trouser

pockets, frowning. He knew why he felt gloomier, too—he knew why the past weekend had been the most depressing of his entire life. On top of everything else, he'd spent the weekend alone. . . missing Billie.

Shoving the thought of Billie from his mind, Steven wandered over to a cluster of Sweet Valley High students. Enid, Olivia, Lila, and Amy were all wearing nice dresses; Winston had on a jacket and tie. They stood with their arms folded, conversing in low, solemn voices. *They look like they're at a funeral,* Steven thought grimly. And maybe, in a way, they were.

"Hey, Steven," Winston said quietly, patting Steven on the shoulder.

Enid gave Steven's hand a reassuring squeeze.

Even Lila's manner was gentle and solicitous. "How *are* you, Steven? I'm really glad to see your mom looking so well. I've been worried about her . . . health."

"Her health?" Steven echoed, reminded—unpleasantly—of his conversation a few days earlier with Bart Lloyd.

Lila glanced at the others, biting her lip. "Well, Jessica told us that she seemed a little . . . shaky," she explained delicately. "Of course, the trial has put a tremendous strain on her—it's *completely* understandable. I just hope she knows—you all know—that if there's *anything* any of us can do . . ."

At that moment, a bell sounded, indicating that court was in session. As he hurried inside with the others to take his seat, Steven mulled over Lila's little speech. Suddenly, it registered. *"Jessica told us . . ."*

Jessica, Steven thought, shaking his head in disbelief as he slipped into a chair next to his loud-mouthed sister. *So she's the one who's been blabbing all over town about Mom's mental state!* Or maybe she only blabbed to Lila and Amy. But, even so, the way those girls gossiped, Steven figured it probably only took about thirty seconds for the rumor of a nervous breakdown to reach the university and Bart Lloyd.

Which means, Steven realized, suddenly feeling sick to his stomach, *maybe Billie didn't have anything to do with this after all.*

Jessica sat bolt upright in her seat, captivated by the scene before her. *So this is what Liz has been up against,* she realized, experiencing an unwanted flicker of compassion. *All these people prying into her life and staring at her as if she were a circus sideshow. . . .*

The judge, Mr. Wakefield, and the prosecuting attorney emerged from the judge's chambers and took their places. Jessica noticed that her father

146

looked more energetic than he had in weeks. He's probably just glad it's almost over, she thought to herself. Steven had told Jessica there would be a few more questions for Elizabeth, after which their father and Mr. Dilworth would make closing statements. And then . . . the judge would render the verdict.

What will it be? Jessica wondered, her heart racing. *Guilty or innocent?* She asked herself another question . . . an even harder question. *What do I want the verdict to be?*

"The state calls Elizabeth Wakefield to the stand."

It sounded like a line from a movie. But this wasn't a movie, Jessica knew; this was real life. And a life—Elizabeth's—was on the line.

She'd thought she could remain detached. She and Elizabeth were estranged from each other; the close bond that had connected them had snapped in two. But as her sister rose to her feet and walked forward, Jessica felt the muscles in her own legs tingle. As Elizabeth placed her hand on the Bible and took an oath to tell the whole truth and nothing but the truth, Jessica's own palms grew damp. When Elizabeth licked her lips, preparing for the interrogation, Jessica discovered that her own mouth was dry. *I should be up there, too,* she recognized, tensing for the prosecutor's first question. *I should be on trial right alongside Elizabeth. . . .*

"Now, Elizabeth," Mr. Dilworth began, his tone cold and snide, in Jessica's opinion. "We're going to go over this one more time, because I know that it's possible in cases of amnesia and blackout for some, if not all, of the lost memory to return at any time. I hope today you have something to share with us."

For what Jessica knew had to be the thousandth time, he proceeded to grill Elizabeth mercilessly about her actions leading up to the crash. "You acknowledge, Elizabeth, that you were drunk at the time of the accident?"

"Yes," said Elizabeth, her voice strained. "I admit I was drunk."

"Let's put together the details, then. Where did you get the liquor? When did you start drinking, and how many alcoholic drinks did you consume?"

"For the last time," said Elizabeth, looking and sounding desperate and weary, "I know it sounds crazy, but I don't *know* how I got the liquor. I know I was drunk because when the police got there, they told me I was—they gave me a breath test. But I—I—" Elizabeth choked on a sob. "I don't know how it happened, I swear. Someone must have spiked my drink or something. . . ."

"Someone must have spiked my drink. . . ." Elizabeth's words acted like an electric prod. Her

148

eyes wide with guilty terror, Jessica sprang to her feet, gripping the bench in front of her. *No!* she wanted to shout in self-defense. *No! You can't prove it!*

"Jessica, sit down!" Alice Wakefield whispered, tugging at Jessica's skirt.

"What?" Jessica asked, a bit too loudly.

People were turning to stare at her. "Sit *down*," her mother hissed.

Jessica allowed her mother to pull her back into her seat, but she continued to lean forward, her hands clasped tightly on her knees. Her nerves were stretched to the breaking point. She simply didn't know if she could trust herself not to leap up again, not to shout out. What was the prosecutor going to say next? What was Elizabeth going to say next?

What if all of a sudden she does *remember?* Jessica wondered, agonized. *What if on some level, deep down inside, she knows it was me?*

But Elizabeth wasn't going to have to answer any more questions. "I have nothing further," Mr. Dilworth declared, turning away.

"You may step down," the judge instructed Elizabeth.

It's over, then, Jessica thought, slumping in her seat with relief. *It's over.*

She looked at her father, expecting to see him

149

slump, too, with despair and defeat. Instead, Ned Wakefield sprang energetically to his feet. "Judge Baird, as per the agreement made earlier this morning, defense would like to call a surprise witness," he announced, his voice booming throughout the courtroom.

A surprise witness? All around her, voices began to buzz excitedly. Her eyes bright with hope, Alice Wakefield reached out to grab Jessica's hand. Jessica's own face drained of all color; the tension returned to her body.

What's happening—what's going on? A surprise witness . . . ? Did someone see me spike Elizabeth's drink? Jessica wondered fearfully. Was her own father going to be the one to unveil her crime to the world?

Leaving the witness stand to walk back to her seat, Elizabeth had nearly fainted. *It's over,* she'd thought, her heart dying inside her and her knees buckling. *It's over.*

Now she stared with unbelieving eyes at her father. Mr. Wakefield glanced at her, and something encouraging in his gaze, something confident, stirred a tiny flame of hope in Elizabeth's heart. Who could it be? What would he or she have to say?

"I'd like to call Gilbert Harding to the stand," Mr. Wakefield stated.

Along with everyone else in the courtroom, Elizabeth twisted in her seat to get a look at the young man who was walking down the aisle. He looked like an ordinary guy, about Steven's age, with a chubby face and white-blond hair. Elizabeth was absolutely sure she'd never seen him before in her life. What could he know about any of this?

Gilbert Harding took the oath and eased himself nervously into his seat on the stand.

"Gilbert, tell the court your full name, age, address, and occupation, please," Mr. Wakefield requested.

"My name is Gil—Gilbert Harding," he said, his voice shaking. "I'm twenty years of age and I live with my parents in Ramsbury, on Royal Palm Road. I'm a student at the community college."

"OK, Gil. Thank you," Mr. Wakefield said. "Now will you tell us where you were and what you were doing at approximately ten-thirty on the night of . . ."

The night of the prom! Elizabeth thought, clasping her hands together tightly in her lap.

Gil took a deep breath. "That night," he began hoarsely, "that night, I drove over to Sweet Valley to visit a friend—a girl I'd been dating. We went out to dinner and got into an argument, a pretty bad one. Right then and there, she decided she wanted to break it off. She took a cab home and I—I got in my car."

"What kind of car was it?" Mr. Wakefield asked.

"A . . . a Buick," Gil replied, his voice faltering.

"Go on," Mr. Wakefield prompted gently. "What happened next?"

Gil ran a trembling hand over his face. "I headed home. I was driving pretty fast. I was pretty upset. And I'd had a few beers. I don't know exactly how it happened—I took my eyes off the road for a second, I guess. And when I looked up—" His voice cracked. "When I looked up, I was coming around a bend on the wrong side of the road, and there was a black Jeep heading straight at me."

Elizabeth put a hand to her throat. She felt herself choke with fear as she must have that night. A car was coming right at her, but there wasn't time to get out of the way! She couldn't avoid it—they were going to crash!

Gil pointed at Elizabeth, his eyes flooding with tears of remorse. "The whole thing was my fault—*she* was driving just fine," he confessed. "She swerved, and I swerved, but it was too late. Probably because I'd been drinking. I sideswiped the Jeep, and it went off the road, and I . . . and I . . ." He dropped his face in his hands. "I panicked and I just kept going. I'm so sorry, Miss Wakefield, Mr. Wakefield," he sobbed. "I'm sorry

I didn't come forward sooner. I'm sorry for what I put you through. I'm guilty of a hit-and-run accident—*I* caused that boy's death. And I'm ready to take my punishment."

"Thank you, Gilbert," Mr. Wakefield said somberly. "No further questions."

An excited murmur raced around the courtroom, and Judge Baird rapped with her gavel to quiet the growing din. "The court will adjourn for fifteen minutes." Despite the judge's proclamation, Elizabeth sat frozen and pale as a statue, her face a mask of disbelief. *Am I dreaming?* she wondered. *Can his story possibly be true—it wasn't my fault, I didn't kill Sam?*

She couldn't take it all in; she simply wasn't able to grasp the full significance of what they had all just heard. Could Gilbert Harding's testimony really mean she wasn't guilty after all? She was going to be allowed to walk out of the courtroom . . . free?

"Because of the evidence just presented to the court," Judge Baird intoned as the court reconvened and the audience listened breathlessly, "I hereby find Elizabeth Wakefield not guilty of the charge of vehicular manslaughter. However," she added, "because she *was* driving while intoxicated, Elizabeth's driver's license will remain suspended for a period

153

to be determined at a later date." With a smile for Elizabeth, the judge slammed down her gavel. "Case closed."

The sudden, shocking turn of events had left Jessica stunned. Now she let out her breath in a long sigh, feeling light-headed. *Elizabeth's off the hook,* Jessica thought with a weird sense of elation. Elizabeth was off the hook . . . and therefore, so was she. Someone else had been guilty all along!

The noise in the courtroom was deafening. Throughout the room, people were jumping to their feet, shouting and gesturing. Jessica watched as her father threw his arms around a limp, shell-shocked Elizabeth, hugging her as if he would never let go. Meanwhile, Mrs. Wakefield embraced Steven, tears of joy running down both their faces. Then the two of them rushed to Elizabeth's side as well.

Jessica leaned forward to look at Todd, who was sitting closer to the aisle next to Enid. He, too, was focusing on Elizabeth, joy and longing written clearly on his face for all the world to see. Turning his back on Jessica, he started toward the aisle . . . toward Elizabeth.

I might as well not even exist, Jessica thought, her elation fading and bitterness once again filling her heart.

The doors to the hallway burst open and members of the press surged into the courtroom. As Elizabeth came up the aisle, flashbulbs started popping. Jessica watched her sister closely waiting to see what Elizabeth might say to Todd . . . or to her.

But Elizabeth didn't even glance their way. She was laughing and crying at the same time, clinging to her mother with one arm and her father with the other, while Steven walked ahead to clear a path. The emotional roller coaster of the last week had left her dazed. She didn't seem to be aware of anything that was going on around her—clearly she was happy just to be with her family, to be going home.

And I guess I'm not a part of the family anymore, Jessica thought, overcome by a sudden sense of almost unbearable loneliness and isolation.

She looked at Todd. He was staring after Elizabeth, his expression guilty and pained. *I have to make him see what I see,* Jessica thought. The trial was over, but nothing had changed. Justice hadn't really been served. Who was going to make reparation to her and Todd for *their* suffering?

Stepping up to Todd's side, Jessica grasped his arm. Slowly, Todd tore his gaze from Elizabeth's retreating figure and turned his head to meet Jessica's cold, hurt eyes.

155

Jessica pressed close to his side, clinging possessively to his arm. "Let's get out of here, Todd," she commanded, holding his gaze, willing him to bend to her wishes, to abandon his misguided dream of a reconciliation with Elizabeth.

Todd's shoulders drooped somewhat; the last faint glimmer of hope flickered out in his eyes. He nodded and, putting his hand over Jessica's, escorted her from the courtroom.

Chapter 11

Having returned to his apartment after the trial, Steven loosened his tie, then yanked it off and tossed it over the back of a chair. His blazer followed suit. Kicking off his good shoes, he padded over to the living room sofa in his socks.

There was a stack of mail to go through, a couple of newspapers he hadn't had time to read, and more than a couple of textbooks he hadn't cracked in days. If he hurried and changed, he could probably catch the second half of the intramural soccer game.

The trial is over—I can get back to my life now, Steven thought. But for some reason he didn't feel like playing sports or doing homework. He didn't feel like calling up any of the friends he hadn't seen in weeks. Because he couldn't just go back to his old routine. True, the trial was over and, miraculously, Elizabeth was free . . . but Billie was gone.

Putting his feet on top of the cedar blanket chest he used as a coffee table, Steven looked around the apartment, noticing all the small changes Billie had made while she was there: the spice rack on the kitchen counter, a row of flowering plants on the windowsill, the big basket she'd bought for them to throw all their sports equipment into—so the apartment wouldn't be permanently cluttered by tennis rackets and basketballs and Frisbees and softball gloves.

When she was here, this place was a real home. Steven smiled, remembering the morning he'd woken up to find Billie in the kitchen, flipping pancakes. *And now . . .*

Now all the little feminine touches only made the apartment seem emptier, lonelier. All Steven could see was what wasn't there—*who* wasn't there. His heart was aching for Billie. He knew she would never walk through his door again.

"I didn't even realize I was falling in love with her," Steven said aloud. "What a dork!" And probably the reason he didn't was that, first and foremost, he considered her such a good *friend*. . . .

Steven winced, remembering their last conversation. Not that you could really call it a conversation—he'd done all the talking, or rather, shouting. *What came over me?* Steven wondered, rubbing his eyes tiredly. Was it just the stress of the trial that caused him to fly off the handle, to be so unforgivably quick to accuse Billie of betraying him and his family? *I was scared—I was totally off balance. And maybe I was feeling even more vulnerable because, on top of everything else, I was falling for her.*

There was no excuse, though, Steven knew. He couldn't believe he'd thought what he thought, and said what he said. Sure, Billie had had the power to hurt him . . . but she never would have, in a million years. All she'd done in the time they'd known each other was look for ways to cheer him up and make him feel better. How could he have been so cruel to her, when she'd been so sensitive and caring when he'd been hurting?

All the time it was Jess who was talking about Mom. Steven shook his head with a sad, cynical smile. *I guess I should have known.*

Just then, the phone rang. Steven leapt to his feet, a jolt of adrenaline causing his heart to pound like a drum solo. *Maybe it's her!* he thought, reaching the phone in two strides.

"Hi—hello," he croaked into the receiver.

"Steven, it's Eve," the voice on the other end

announced brightly. "I just wanted to remind you that the prelaw study group is meeting at my place tomorrow night, and it's your turn to bring the snacks. Unless tonight would be better for you—we're flexible."

All the hopeful energy drained from Steven's body. "No, I'm driving back down to Sweet Valley for dinner tonight. I'll be there tomorrow," he promised, without much enthusiasm. "See ya."

"Bye."

Steven hung up the phone. For a long moment, he stood leaning against the kitchen counter, thinking. He knew he was lucky to have buddies like Eve. They'd always be there for him, through good times and bad—he could count on it. But *love* . . . love was something else again. You had to grab love while you had the chance. Steven thought about what he'd said to Todd the day Todd came to his apartment for advice about Elizabeth. *I really told him off,* Steven recalled, smiling grimly. *Boy, talk about the pot calling the kettle black!* He'd accused Todd of failing to have faith in Elizabeth . . . then he'd gone and made the same mistake with Billie.

And I probably totally discouraged Todd from trying to patch things up with Liz, Steven thought remorsefully. *I sure hope he didn't listen to me!*

Because maybe if Todd tried to talk to Elizabeth, to explain things to her, and maybe if *he* tried to talk to Billie, to explain things to *her* . . .

Yes, Steven decided, his spirits lifting. *I owe it to her . . . and to myself.*

"Well, the trial's over," Lila said to Amy as she turned the car key in the ignition. "Case closed, *finis*. Into the history books it goes."

She backed her lime-green Triumph out of the parking spot in front of the little restaurant where they'd grabbed a sandwich after leaving the courthouse. As they headed down Main Street, Amy rolled down her window, shaking her blond hair in the breeze. "Thank goodness," Amy remarked. "But do you think this'll ever really be *over* for the Wakefields? I mean, honestly—how can Liz just go back to normal life at school? And what about Jessica?"

"Jessica's a basket case," Lila had to agree. "Why on *earth* is she chasing after Todd Wilkins? What's going through her mind?"

"I have no idea," Amy admitted. "I have absolutely no idea."

"Well, maybe *some* things'll get a little better, now that the trial's over," Lila said optimistically. "Maybe she'll start talking to us again."

Amy sighed. "I hope so. Oh, hey, that reminds me," she added. "Speaking of talking, do you mind if we stop at Project Youth on the way home? I need to type up next month's Teen Hotline operator schedule. It'll only take a few minutes." Amy shot a glance at Lila. "I mean, you don't feel uncomfortable going in there, do you? Because you *could* just wait in the car. . . ."

"Not at all," Lila declared. "I'm not seeing Nathan for counseling anymore, but we're on perfectly good terms—we got everything straightened out. In fact, I was thinking that maybe I should become a volunteer, too. I'd probably be pretty good at the hotline thing," Lila smiled at Amy. "I've sure had enough experience talking on the telephone!" She signaled for a right turn. "Let's go!"

I really do *feel OK about this place*, Lila thought a few minutes later, as she and Amy strolled through the door of the Community Center into the offices where Project Youth was located. *It's amazing what a person can work through.*

Amy elbowed Lila in the side, breaking into her thoughts. "Hey, Li—look who's here!" she whispered.

Lila turned to see Pamela Robertson standing at the front desk, talking to the receptionist. Pamela glanced in their direction, but when she saw Lila and Amy staring at her, she looked away quickly, her cheeks flushing.

"I wonder what she's doing here?" Amy murmured as they went into the room where the typewriter was.

Through the open door, Lila watched as Pamela ducked into a room on the other side of the corridor, closing the door behind her. "I don't know. I hope she's not here for counseling. She looks like such a nice girl. I'd feel terrible if, after only a week at Sweet Valley High, she needed therapy!"

"Tell me about it," said Amy, making a rueful face. "I feel like a total witch for blabbing about her reputation. Thanks to my big mouth, Bruce trashed their relationship." She shook her head. "And he was really crazy about her."

"She really hasn't gotten a fair shot," Lila agreed. "You know, with this whole reputation thing . . ."

Lila didn't have to think very hard to remember a time when her own reputation was on the line—when she was telling one story about what happened between her and John Pfeifer on their infamous date, and he was telling another.

"How much do any of us really know about Pamela, anyway?" Lila wondered out loud. "I mean, has anybody actually *talked* to her, tried to get to *know* her? Or have we all just assumed that her 'reputation' tells us everything we need to know?"

"I haven't said a single word to her," Amy confessed remorsefully. "So much for the sensitivity I've supposedly learned being a Project Youth volunteer!" She bit her lip. "What do you think, Li? Is it too late to try to make it up to her, maybe even get her and Bruce back together?"

Lila narrowed her eyes, gazing at Pamela. She thought about Gil Harding in the courtroom, coming forward at the last minute to accept the blame for the car crash and Sam's death; she thought about her mother, flying halfway around the world to be with her, after sixteen years of silence. "No," Lila said at last. "It's not too late. It's *never* too late."

"These are the children you'll be working with, Pamela," said Carla, the coordinator of Project Youth's after-school program for kids whose parents worked. "Danny Lee, Rosita DeAngelis, Billy Barstow, Jane Piper, and Amanda Horowitz." Carla smiled at the five children. "And this is Pamela Robertson," she told them. "She's a junior at Sweet Valley High, and she'll be with you on Tuesdays and Fridays, starting tomorrow."

"We're eight years old," Billy told Pamela. "How old is a junior?"

Pamela smiled. "Sixteen. That makes me twice as old as you!"

Rosita wrinkled her freckled nose. "Wow, that's

old. Are you sure you can keep up with us if we go to the park to play games?"

Pamela laughed. "I'll sure try. I'll wear my track shoes!"

"I think you'll all get along famously," Carla predicted, winking at Pamela. "OK, don't forget, all the arts and crafts supplies need to be put back in the cupboard before you go home. Pamela will help you."

This is going to be fun, Pamela mused as she helped stow away boxes of crayons, colored paper, and Popsicle sticks. *Too bad it's only two days a week!* It was better than nothing, though, and if she was lucky, maybe it would lead to other volunteer responsibilities at Project Youth. *At least I'll keep a little busier, feel a little more involved,* Pamela thought. She had to do *something* with her spare time, and her experience trying out for the tennis team—or more accurately, her run-in with Bruce in the parking lot afterward—had been so demoralizing, she knew it would be quite a while before she got up the nerve to go out for any other Sweet Valley High extracurricular activities.

Speaking of Sweet Valley High . . . As she put away the last pair of child-sized scissors, Pamela darted a glance into the hallway. She really hoped those two girls from school weren't still around. . . .

Pamela said good-bye to the little kids and

stepped back out into the reception area. And there they were, pushpinning a chart of some sort to the Project Youth bulletin board. *Amy what's-her-name, the cheerleader,* Pamela recognized, *and that rich girl—the one whose father owns the computer chip company. Fowler—Lila Fowler.*

The girls caught sight of Pamela at the same moment that she caught sight of them. They stared across the lobby at her, and then, putting their heads close together, started whispering furiously.

Pamela turned away, desperately looking for an escape route, someplace to hide. A childish voice provided a welcome distraction. "Mommy, here she is," Pamela heard Jane Piper chirp. "Here's my new after-school teacher!"

Holding Jane by one hand, Mrs. Piper extended the other hand to Pamela. "It's nice to meet you," she said warmly. "I know you only just started, but Jane tells me she likes you already."

Squatting down, Pamela gave Jane a big smile. "I like you, too, Jane."

"See you tomorrow," the little girl called as she tagged after her mother toward the door.

"You bet!" Pamela called back.

Still smiling, she straightened up, pivoting on her heel . . . to find Amy and Lila standing right behind her.

Pamela's smile faded and she blushed profusely.

"Excuse me," she muttered, hurrying to get out of their path.

"Pamela, wait," Amy said. "Lila and I were just wondering . . ." Now it was Amy's turn to blush. "Well, we were just wondering—if you're done here, if you'd like to get a soda with us."

Pamela gaped at them, speechless. Where on earth was *this* coming from? Lila and Amy were two of the most popular girls at Sweet Valley High. Why would they bother with *her*, knowing what they did about her?

They must have an ulterior motive, Pamela suspected. *They're going to set me up—make fun of me, pull some kind of prank.* So far, only one other person from Sweet Valley High had made a friendly overture toward her, and Pamela had blown him off; she knew Roger Barrett Patman was Bruce's cousin, and with the way Bruce was treating her these days, she hadn't trusted *Roger's* motives, either.

But maybe she'd been mistaken, Pamela acknowledged now. *Maybe Roger* was *just trying to be nice.* As for Lila and Amy, what did she have to lose? She might as well give them the benefit of the doubt. If they turned out to be catty and mean, well, she could handle it. And if not . . . maybe she'd finally have a friend or two in Sweet Valley.

Lila had picked up on her hesitation—it would

have been hard not to. "We were thinking about the Box Tree Café," she elaborated, flashing Pamela a brilliant, magnanimous smile. "My treat."

"You should really accept the offer," Amy advised a still tongue-tied Pamela. "Take it from someone who knows—it'll probably never happen again!"

Lila pouted; Pamela couldn't help laughing. "Well . . . OK," she said shyly.

"Great!" Amy took Pamela's arm. "C'mon, we're parked right out front."

Jessica pushed the food around on her plate, feeling sick to her stomach. She hadn't eaten a bite, and she didn't plan to. *Salmon with dill sauce—yuck*, she thought sourly. *Mom knows I hate salmon, but she made it anyway because* Elizabeth *loves it, and this is* Elizabeth's *celebration dinner.*

No one else at the table seemed to be aware of Jessica's less than congenial mood. Her mother, her father, Steven, Elizabeth . . . they were all giddy, laughing at the least little thing, bubbling over with happiness.

"I still can't believe it," Elizabeth said, shaking her head. "In just a few minutes, my whole life turned around. I'm still dizzy!"

"Me, too," said Mrs. Wakefield. She gazed at

her daughter, her eyes shining. "I feel like a butter-fly that's just come out of its chrysalis. I feel *alive* again, after all these weeks of hiding out and being afraid because there was nothing I could do to protect you from what was happening to you."

Tears filling her eyes, Elizabeth bent forward to kiss her mother's cheek.

Mr. Wakefield reached out to squeeze Mrs. Wakefield's hand. "Welcome back," he murmured, his voice gruff with emotion.

Elizabeth dabbed at her eyes with her napkin. "You *did* help me, though, Mom," she insisted. "You *all* helped me so much, just by being there." Jessica couldn't help noticing that Elizabeth looked around the table at everyone but her. "I couldn't have made it without you." Elizabeth sniffled. "I'm just so lucky to be part of this family!"

"That's what families are for," Steven declared, his own eyes damp. "When everything else is falling apart, your family will always be there for you. We would never have let you face something like this on your own."

"Let's remember this moment, this closeness," Mr. Wakefield proposed, raising his water glass in a toast. "Let's remember this feeling and never let go of it."

Elizabeth, Steven, and Mrs. Wakefield all lifted their glasses. Suddenly, Jessica couldn't bear it—

she couldn't sit there for one second more. *"Let's remember this feeling, and never let go of it . . ." Is he kidding? Doesn't anyone know how I'm feeling? Doesn't anyone care that my torment hasn't lessened one bit?* Jessica couldn't stop thinking that, despite the fact that somebody else had caused the car crash, it was she who had spiked the drinks. If it weren't for her, Sam and Elizabeth would never have taken off like that, thoughtlessly putting themselves in the path of harm—of death.

Jessica shoved back her chair, jumping to her feet. "I don't *want* to remember this moment," she burst out. "It's not happy—it's horrible! How can you sit there and act like just because Liz was found innocent, everything's perfect, everything's fixed?"

"Jessica," Ned Wakefield began gently. "We know—"

"No, you *don't* know," Jessica cried. "You don't *care*. All you care about is Elizabeth. Well, maybe the stupid trial is over—" Her voice broke on a sob; she was blinded by tears of fury, and sorrow, and bewilderment. "But Sam is still dead!"

Whirling, Jessica ran from the room, her family staring after her in silence.

Chapter 12

Elizabeth and Enid paused for a moment on Tuesday outside the door to the cafeteria. All at once, Elizabeth's courage deserted her. Going to classes that morning had been one thing, but entering the lunchroom and facing the entire Sweet Valley High student body. . . . "I don't know if I can do this," she whispered.

Enid slipped an arm around Elizabeth's waist, giving her friend a quick, hard hug. "Yes, you can," she declared. "I'm right here beside you. And remember, everyone's happy for you, and happy to have you back in school. You're not on trial anymore, Liz."

Enid's right, Elizabeth told herself. *It's time to*

put all that behind me and move on. I've been given a second chance, and I have to go for it—I have to make a new start.

She took a deep breath, smiling weakly at Enid. "OK, I'm ready."

As usual, the noise level in the Sweet Valley High cafeteria was deafening. Did it drop a decibel or two as she walked in? Elizabeth wasn't sure. *But so what if people are talking about me*, she thought. After everything she'd been through, after being hounded by the press for weeks, a few more stares and a little more gossip wasn't going to hurt her!

They made their way to a table in the far corner where Olivia, Penny, and DeeDee were already seated.

"Liz, it's so good to see you!" Olivia exclaimed, reaching out to squeeze Elizabeth's arm.

"It's *fantastic*," DeeDee asserted. "It just wasn't the same around here without you."

"Tell me about it." Penny flashed Elizabeth a wry, affectionate smile. "We weren't able to put together a single decent issue of *The Oracle* while you were gone!"

Elizabeth laughed, the welcoming words and smiles bringing her perilously close to tears. "I've missed you guys, too." She pulled out a chair and sank into it gratefully. "This hasn't been the easiest day, but I'm getting through it, thanks to all of you."

"Well, you can relax now," Olivia assured her. "You're among friends. So just sit back and eat your lunch!"

Among friends . . . Elizabeth ducked her head to hide her tear-bright eyes. What a difference it made, having friends!

As the other girls began discussing the likelihood that Ms. Dalton would postpone the French exam, Elizabeth thought about how her friends had stood by her during her troubles, checking in with her by telephone, showing their support by sitting in on the trial. . . .

Elizabeth's eyes flickered to another table not far away. Todd was watching her, as she was aware he had been ever since she entered the lunchroom.

Elizabeth shifted her chair, turning her back to him. *I can't look at him,* she thought, hunching her shoulders protectively. *I can't* think *about him. It's just too much.*

She focused on eating her sandwich, basking in the comfort of her friends' idle conversation. It was all she wanted right now—all she felt capable of dealing with. If she thought about Todd, if she opened that door, she knew all her guilty feelings would tumble out and crush her. And she wasn't strong enough to confront them—not yet.

Elizabeth shivered at the thought of Todd sitting in court day in and day out, hearing over and over again the incomplete but still repulsive story of her drunkenness, her recklessness, of how she ditched her own boyfriend to take off with her sister's, driving away with him, delivering him to his death even if she didn't cause it directly.

He must think I'm a monster, Elizabeth supposed. *And I was a monster that night. I don't deserve him. It's right that he should stay away from me, that he should forget all about me and find someone new, someone worthy of him.*

For a moment, Elizabeth had to squeeze her eyes tightly shut. Thinking about Todd with another girl—maybe even with Jessica—made her want to cry, to tear out her hair and sob. She missed him so much it hurt. *But it's over between us,* Elizabeth reminded herself. *Todd loved me in another life. That was then, before; this is now, after. I—we—can never go back. . . .*

"Liz, are you OK?"

Elizabeth blinked. Enid, Penny, Olivia, and DeeDee were staring at her, concerned.

Elizabeth nodded, forcing a halfhearted smile. "Sorry, I just spaced out for a minute there. What were you guys talking about?"

"The newspaper," Penny replied. "I was just about to ask you if you think you'd have time to write an article about the art history field trip this week as well as your usual column."

"Sure, I'd be happy to," Elizabeth said eagerly.

This was exactly what she wanted: to fill every waking hour with school and homework and writing. It was the only way she was going to survive. Because Elizabeth knew that if she really wanted to make a fresh start, she had to cut her losses. And maybe if she threw herself back into her work, it would ease the pain of knowing that her twin sister hated her . . . maybe it would even help her forget the only boy she'd ever loved.

Late Tuesday afternoon, Bruce slammed his gym locker shut and grabbed his sport bag. *I won't bump into her today,* he guessed, whistling tunelessly through his teeth as he headed for the door. It looked as if Pamela had given up on the idea of trying out for the tennis team. In fact, Bruce got the impression she'd given up on a *lot* of things; he hardly saw her around at all anymore. *She got the message—she's avoiding me,* he speculated, not sure whether he felt relief or disappointment . . . not sure whether he'd even sent the right message in the first place.

He emerged from the men's locker room—and practically stepped on a girl waiting right outside the door. Amy flashed him a bright smile. "Hi, Bruce!"

"What are *you* doing here?" Bruce grumbled, running a hand through his damp hair.

"I just finished cheerleading practice," Amy explained. "And try to contain your enthusiasm, Bruce," she added dryly. "I know you're thrilled to see me."

Bruce shrugged apologetically. "Sorry. It's nothing personal—I've just been in a lousy mood lately."

Amy smiled. "I'll say!" They started walking down the sidewalk together. "Listen, can I bum a ride home from you?" she asked. "Barry borrowed my car to run an errand."

Bruce cocked one eyebrow. Any one of the cheerleaders could give Amy a ride, and didn't Barry have his own car? It sounded a *little* contrived. *What does she want from me?* Bruce wondered, and then realized he didn't care. Besides, he could use the company. He shrugged again. "Sure. No problem."

"How's the tennis team these days?" Amy asked as they climbed into the Porsche. She chattered on without waiting for an answer. "Cheerleading's going really well—we have all new cheers for the next pep rally. Of course, Jessica's in a foul mood these days—even worse than yours—so Robin's pretty much running everything, which makes *some* of us think that maybe it's time for Jess to step down as co-captain and let someone else have a shot at it for a while. I mean, it would be only fair, right?"

Amy paused to take a breath. Bruce shot a glance at her out of the corner of his eye. *Does Barry ever get a word in edgewise?* he wondered, suppressing a smile.

"I'm seriously considering advising Jess to go to Project Youth for counseling," Amy went on. "First I have to think of the right way to bring up the subject, though—I don't want to offend her or make her mad or scare her off or anything. And *speaking* of Project Youth, you'll *never* guess who's volunteering there now. Pamela Robertson!"

Surprised by the introduction of Pamela's name, Bruce hit the gas, and then just as abruptly slammed on the brake when he saw the traffic light at the upcoming intersection turn yellow.

"Yep," said Amy, "Pam Robertson. She's working with little kids in an after-school program. And that's really why I'm here, Bruce—I just wanted to apologize for gossiping about her. I did her a disfavor . . . I did a *lot* of people a disfavor."

Bruce drummed his fingers on the steering wheel. "Well, you didn't really say anything that wasn't true," he mumbled.

"But I did," Amy insisted, twisting in her seat and fixing him with a pair of incredibly sincere slate-gray eyes. "I didn't know her at all when I said those things. Now I've spent some time with her, and she's a great person—really caring, and fun, and smart. I mean, you can't judge a book by its cover, you know? Take me, for example."

The light changed and Bruce sped forward. "Yeah, what about you?"

"You might not believe this, but some people think I'm just an airhead," said Amy.

Bruce laughed. "No way! Why would they think that?"

Amy punched him in the arm. "The point is, I'm *not* an airhead, and anyone who actually *knows* me knows that. The same goes for you."

Bruce lifted his eyebrows. "Me?"

"Yeah. If I didn't *know* you, if I just went on the basis of your *reputation*, I'd assume you were a cocky, selfish, spoiled, arrogant heartbreaker."

"But I'm not, right?"

"Well, there's another side to you, anyway," Amy teased.

They both burst out laughing.

"Seriously, though," she continued, "I've learned a lot answering the hotline at Project Youth. I've learned how much you miss if you don't *listen* to people, if you forget that everybody has his or her own story, and the only way to find out what it is is to let them tell it."

Amy was being unbelievably nosy and pre-sumptuous; Bruce really couldn't believe he had let her get away with bringing up the subject of Pamela. But he couldn't help smiling at this goody-good, do-unto-others rhetoric, especially coming from Amy. "What an inspirational speech," he kidded. "Next thing we know, you'll be handing out pamphlets at the airport."

"Well, I meant every word."

They'd reached Amy's street. Bruce coasted to a stop in front of her house. "So long," he said.

Amy put her hand on the door handle. Before getting out, though, she turned back toward him. "One more thing you should know, Bruce," she said quietly. "Pamela's still in love with you."

With that, Amy hopped out of the car and slammed the door behind her, leaving Bruce wondering, a softened look in his brooding, dark eyes.

"It's really cute. I'm tempted," Pamela confessed on Wednesday afternoon, eyeing the red-and-black checked miniskirt Amy was dangling in front of her. "But . . ." She shook her head. "I already spent my whole clothes allowance this month. I'll have to pass."

"I was hoping you'd say that!" exclaimed Lila, snatching the skirt from Amy. "It will look great with my new red body suit. Ring this up, please," she commanded, tossing the skirt to a passing salesclerk.

"Some people don't *have* clothes allowances," Amy explained to Pamela as they watched Lila flipping through a thick stack of credit cards. "The sky's the limit for Li. I just go along for the vicarious thrills."

Pamela smiled. "It's just as well—it'll look better on her, anyway."

Lila smiled broadly. "Oh, I *like* this girl!"

Lila's purchase in hand, the three girls left the boutique laughing. *I can't believe this is really me,* Pamela thought as they strolled through the Mall, browsing idly. She couldn't help smiling: a dizzy, happy, optimistic smile. She felt like a different person. She wasn't alone; she had friends.

"Let's stop here," Pamela suggested as they came abreast of Casey's Ice Cream Parlor. "My treat this time."

They stepped up to the counter to read the list of flavors. "Dishes or cones?" asked Pamela. "Should we sit down for a minute or keep walking?"

"Dishes," Lila opted. "Fewer calories that way."

A minute later they were seated at a little table in the corner with their ice cream. Amy raised her eyebrows. "Fewer *calories*?" she said, looking pointedly at Lila's hot-fudge sundae. "Don't you think the sauce and the nuts and the whipped cream sort of cancel out any advantage you might have had by giving up the cone?"

Lila grinned. "Don't you think *you* should be quiet?"

They dug in. "Umm." Amy licked her spoon. "Casey's is the best."

"It is," agreed Pamela. "I've been here before, actually." She lowered her eyes. "With Bruce."

Lila and Amy exchanged glances. "Oh, well . . ." Amy murmured, making a vaguely sympathetic noise.

"It's OK," Pamela assured her. "I don't mind talking about him. I mean, listen to me!" She laughed wryly. "For the first time in weeks, I can say his name without bursting into tears!"

"Sounds like real progress," Lila commented.

"I guess I've just gotten to the point where I can see the light at the end of the tunnel." Pamela leaned her elbows on the table. "These last few days—thanks to you two—I've started to feel stronger, more sure of myself. I can honestly say I still think I made the right move, transferring to Sweet Valley High." Her voice trembled, but only a tiny bit. "It'll be OK even if things don't work out with Bruce." *Even though I'll never stop loving him. . . .* "I'll survive."

"You'll do better than that, Pamela," Amy predicted confidently, with another knowing look at

Lila. "You'll find your niche—you'll be a star."

Pamela sat up straighter. She tossed back her unruly mane of hair. "You're right," she said, smiling. "I will."

Margo stood in the center of the Valley Mall, her bag at her feet. Slowly, she pivoted on her boot heel, drinking it all in. *I'm here,* she thought, her gray eyes shining with a triumphant light. *I'm finally* here!

The time-consuming detour to San Diego had been worth it, Margo decided. It had postponed her arrival at her final destination, but this way she knew she was home free. No one had followed her to Sweet Valley; she'd erased all her trails, cut all the strings that tied her to her old life. Already, even though she'd only been in town for an hour, she felt different, as if she'd been reborn. *I'm starting a brand-new life!* Margo thought, grabbing her bag. *And now it's time to pick up a few essentials. . . .*

She strolled in the direction of Lytton & Brown, a department store, taking her time, enjoying the scenery. On the way, she passed a small group of girls about her own age coming out of an ice cream parlor.

Margo studied them from afar, her gaze both curious and coolly objective. One girl was slim and elegant, with long, glossy brown hair and an outfit that looked casual but had probably cost a fortune; another was dramatically pretty, with pale skin, wild dark hair, and bright blue eyes; the third girl was a gorgeous California blonde with legs about a mile long.

As Margo walked by them—so close, she could have reached out and touched them—she overheard a few words that stopped her dead in her tracks. ". . . Elizabeth Wakefield . . . Sweet Valley High . . ."

The laughing, chattering girls continued on, Margo staring after them. *Sweet Valley High . . . those girls are part of my new life, too!* she realized, thrilled. She'd be their friend soon; soon, all of Sweet Valley would adore her, fight for her favor. *But that tall, blond one,* Margo thought resentfully, *she's too pretty, too perfect. She might have to go.*

Margo sauntered into Lytton and Brown, humming to herself. A saleswoman accosted her immediately. "May I help you, miss?"

Margo blinked, startled. *Why is she looking at me like that? What does she want?*

"Are you shopping for anything in particular?" the woman pressed, her smile ingratiating.

Margo relaxed. "No, thank you, I'm just looking."

She wandered on, scoping out the store with

hungry, practiced eyes. *I could really use a couple of new tank tops,* she thought, pausing to flick a silk scarf from a rack and quickly stuff it into her jacket pocket. *And I wonder if they sell wigs here?* As she strolled past the costume jewelry counter, snatching a bracelet from the display as she went, Margo smiled to herself. *I'm going to like Sweet Valley!*

Chapter 13

Lila pushed aside the straps of her new underwire bikini, baring her shoulders to the warm afternoon sun. "I'm so glad tomorrow is Friday," she remarked to her mother, who was reclining on the chaise lounge next to hers. "It's going to be a really fun weekend. Daddy said he'd try to get tickets to the ballet for Saturday night. Wouldn't that be great?"

"Hmm," Grace murmured.

"And I invited my new friend Pamela to come over for brunch on Sunday. You'll really like her," Lila promised. "She just transferred to Sweet Valley High. She was having a lot of social problems at her old school, so she decided to switch schools—to make a brand-new start. I think that's really gutsy, don't you?"

"It is," Mrs. Fowler agreed.

"Maybe I should ask Jessica over, too," Lila mused. "She's still moping like crazy—she hardly ever leaves the house. Or maybe I should just leave her alone for a while, let her have time to herself if that's what she needs. What do you think, Mom? Mom?" she repeated when her mother didn't respond.

Mrs. Fowler blinked. "I'm sorry, honey. What were you saying?"

"It doesn't matter." Lila studied her mother's face. "Mom . . . are you OK?" she asked quietly.

Her mother gave her a brief smile. "I'm fine. I'm just a little . . . preoccupied. That's all."

"What are you thinking about?" Lila prompted.

Grace shifted sideways in her chair, facing her daughter. "I'm thinking about what happens next," she confessed. "You know, Lila, when I left Paris I left a lot of work behind. I left my home, my job . . . my life. Not that I regret coming here to be with you," she added, putting out a hand to touch Lila's cheek. "No, when your father called, there was no question in my mind that my place was here, with you. But now . . ."

Lila's eyes lit up, her heart flooding with joy. *I was right! There* are *sparks rekindling between*

Mom and Dad! At first, she'd thought it was too much to hope for, that her parents might actually get together again. She'd figured she would just work on persuading her mother to move back to the States, specifically to Southern California. But now . . .

"But now that you've spent some time here with Daddy and me," Lila said eagerly, "you don't want to leave, right?"

Mrs. Fowler bit her lip. "No," she admitted, after a long moment. "No, I don't want to leave. But it's not as simple as that, Lila."

"Why not?" Lila wanted to know. "Why can't you just move back to Sweet Valley and live with—"

"Ssh." Sitting up, Mrs. Fowler swung her slender legs over the side of the chaise. "Lila," she said, taking both her daughter's hands, "maybe it's time you knew the truth about your father and me."

Lila stiffened. She wasn't at all certain that she did want to hear the truth. And her mother's solemn tone scared her. *The truth can't be good, if she talks about it like that*, Lila guessed. But it would be worse to remain in the dark, ignorant about her parents' past. "The . . . the truth?" she said, her voice quavering.

Grace Fowler took a deep breath. "I was very young when I met your father," she began. "He was twenty-seven, but I was only nineteen. He . . ."

She smiled, blushing slightly. "He was my first love. Well, we were very impetuous—we decided to get married after knowing each other for less than two months. Just about everybody we knew tried to talk us out of it."

"How come?" Lila wondered. "Just because of the difference in your ages?"

"No, that was only part of it. The major problem, really, was that we came from very different backgrounds. As you know, your father wasn't raised with money." Grace waved a hand, indicating the sumptuous grounds of Fowler Crest. "All this he created himself. My family, meanwhile, was what was known then as 'old money.' My father didn't even have to work, and George's father was a butcher." She laughed, her eyes crinkling. "I bet you didn't know that!"

Lila was dumbfounded. "No, I didn't."

"Well, I guess it's a classic story. Boy meets girl, but he's from the wrong side of the tracks. They rebel against the disapproval of their families and society, idealistically believing love conquers all."

Lila frowned. She knew what was coming. "It doesn't?"

Grace shook her head sadly. "No, it doesn't. True love can overcome a lot of barriers, but sometimes there are just too many challenges at one time, too many stumbling blocks. That's the way it was for me and George. We hadn't been married very long when we started to have problems. He felt threatened by all the money in my family and set out to make his own. He thought that was what I wanted, when all I really wanted was to be with him, to be a family. But he worked constantly, nonstop. I began to feel like I wasn't even married—I saw him so infrequently. And when he was home we'd fight. Boy, did we shoot off some fireworks! Eventually I started turning away, going back to my family and old friends for company and advice, and so *he* felt hurt and excluded. Finally, when you were still a very small baby, I threatened to leave him. I was desperately unhappy and just couldn't raise you in an atmosphere like that."

Lila sat very still, trying to imagine the scene. "God, what did he do?"

"He begged me to stay. He promised he'd change—that everything would change. But I'd made up my mind. Maybe I didn't know much, but I knew people didn't change, just like that, overnight. If nothing else, we needed a break from each other. So, I packed my bags, and I packed *you*, and I went back to my parents' house."

"But . . ." Lila knew that couldn't be the end of the story. Because her *father* had raised her, not her mother. "What happened then?"

"Your father came after me, and he gave me an

ultimatum. Either I came home with him, or . . . or . . ." Grace faltered, momentarily overcome with emotion. "Or he'd take you away from me. He'd use his newly acquired money, power, and influence to have me legally declared an unfit mother."

Lila's jaw dropped. "He *said* that?"

"He said it, and he did it." Mrs. Fowler's face grew pale; her eyes were pained and distant. "When I insisted on a separation, he made good on his threat. He took me to court and I lost custody of you—I was even denied visiting rights. It was devastating," she said quietly. "But I wouldn't go crawling back to him the way he wanted me to. Instead, I ran in the other direction—all the way to Europe."

Lila was shocked down to her very core. In a million years, she'd never imagined anything like *this*. She didn't know whose behavior was more incomprehensible, more unforgivable, her father's or her mother's. "But how could you?" she whispered, gulping down the tears. "I understand . . . I suppose . . . how you could leave *him*. But how could you leave *me*?"

Grace shook her head. "Maybe part of me believed the things he accused me of. The custody hearing was so demoralizing, so disorienting. And even though what your father did to me was horrible, I knew he loved *you* with all his heart. I knew you'd be brought up with everything a little girl could want."

Everything a little girl could want, Lila reflected. *Sure, every* thing. *But no mother.* It hadn't been a fair trade.

"You were in good hands with him," Grace continued. "You see, in a strange twist of fate my family lost almost all their money soon after you were born. So there I was, with no money, no education, no job skills—nothing. Eventually, I acquired all those things. I learned to be assertive and independent; I learned not to be intimidated by other people's power, not to let myself be bullied. I guess I finally grew up. But it took a long time." She looked deep into her daughter's eyes. "I always vowed I'd return to you, though, Lila—someday, somehow."

Lila shook her head, still struggling to untangle the threads of the story, and to clarify her own mixed feelings. "How could Daddy be so *cruel?*" she asked, unable to reconcile the picture her mother had painted with her own knowledge of her father.

"Please don't blame him," Grace said softly. "You can't know what he was like way back then—what *I* was like. Just remember, the important thing is that he called me—he brought me home to you. He did that because he loves you very much. It took a lot of courage."

Lila smiled through her tears. "And it took a lot of courage for you to come."

Grace Fowler clasped her daughter's hand tightly. "You bet it did. I was terrified at the prospect of seeing you—my little baby Lila, a teenager! I had no idea what you'd heard about me, what your fa—what you'd been told. What if you hated me? I wouldn't have blamed you if you did. Nevertheless, I couldn't stay away—that simply wasn't an option. You're my one and only daughter. And no matter what happened, or what *may* happen, George is the father of my child."

Grace gave Lila's hand one more squeeze and then drew back, reclining once more in her chair. The story was over, Lila reflected. But then again, maybe it wasn't. . . .

A tiny smile played over Lila's lips; her eyes grew dreamy, but also determined. *It may be a long shot, but I'm going to reunite this family,* she vowed silently. Even if they didn't realize it themselves, Lila knew her parents were falling in love again, and she didn't intend to let them blow it this time. She was sick and tired of being Lila Fowler, poor little rich girl. She was going to have a happy family whether her parents liked it or not, and she had a feeling they were going to like it.

*   *   *

I wonder if Elizabeth stuck around after school today, Todd thought as he strode idly down the deserted hallway after basketball practice on Thursday. *Maybe she's catching up on her work at* The Oracle. . . .

Instead of taking the shortest route straight from the gym to the parking lot, Todd was cutting through the high school toward the main lobby. He hadn't consciously decided to go by a route that made it possible he'd run into Elizabeth, but now he had to admit to himself that he was doing just that. *And there's a pretty good chance,* he wagered as he neared the newspaper office.

Maybe there was *too* good a chance. Suddenly, Todd's heart was pounding harder than it had during the workout he'd just completed. What if he *did* bump into Elizabeth? What would he do—what would he say? It had been a week since he'd poured out his heart in the letter he'd delivered to her house, and so far he hadn't received any response—not the sign he'd asked for, not a word, not a glance. They saw each other at school every day, but it was only too obvious Elizabeth was avoiding any contact with him; whenever he looked at her, trying to catch her eye, she turned away.

It wouldn't be a good idea, catching her off guard, Todd decided. *Forget it.* Changing course abruptly, he ducked into the nearest stairwell . . .

and bumped right into Elizabeth, who was just about to open the door from the other side.

"Oh!" Elizabeth said in a high-pitched voice, startled. "Oh, I—excuse—"

"Sorry," said Todd, trying to sidestep out of her way and feeling like a clumsy, oversized oaf. "I was just . . ."

They stood for a moment, not knowing where to look. When Todd dared to look into Elizabeth's soft, clear eyes, he felt his heart breaking. He knew he was totally unworthy of her. He'd been a jerk— he'd abandoned her, he'd gotten involved with her sister. He knew he didn't deserve her, but he wanted her back so badly! *Couldn't she tell that from my letter?* Todd thought in anguish. *Doesn't she know I'd do* anything *to make it up to her? Why doesn't she say something?*

Maybe if he mentioned the letter . . . Todd opened his mouth to speak, and then closed it again, remembering what Jessica had told him. She ripped it up and threw it away. If she wanted to talk about the relationship, she would, but obviously she didn't.

"Well . . . I was just on my way home from practice," he said lamely.

"Of course," Elizabeth responded quickly. "I've got to—"

She pointed toward the door. Todd held it open for her and she hurried off.

He let the door swing shut again, stood alone for a moment in the empty stairwell, then pounded his fist against the wall. It was the closest he'd been to Elizabeth in weeks, and it might as well have been an encounter between total strangers. Bitter disappointment flooded his heart. Elizabeth still hadn't given him the sign that would let him know she was willing to forgive him. And more and more, Todd was starting to believe she never would.

Bruce shuffled down the sidewalk on his way to the parking lot, his chin on his chest and his hands shoved deep in the pockets of his khakis. Once again, tennis team practice had been a total waste of time. It didn't matter that Pamela wasn't playing on the next court; he still couldn't concentrate. It didn't matter that he never saw her or spoke to her; he still thought about her—all the time.

Bruce kicked a pebble with the toe of his tennis shoe, smiling crookedly to himself. *And to think that, of all people, bubble-headed Amy Sutton was the one who set me straight*, he thought, bemused. *It just goes to show, shallow waters run deep, or something like that*.

Bruce thought back to his conversation with Amy . . . or rather, to Amy's monologue. What was that she'd said—about how you had to listen to

195

people if you wanted to learn their story? *I sure didn't listen to Pamela,* Bruce reflected. *I saw something, and I heard some rumors, and I made a judgment, just like that. I never gave her a fair hearing.*

It was kind of like Elizabeth Wakefield's trial, or anybody's trial for that matter, Bruce decided. You couldn't convict people of crimes without giving them a chance to defend themselves. That wasn't justice. *And since when am I qualified to judge anybody, anyway? Like I'm such a saint myself!*

Now that he thought about it, Bruce realized that Pamela's lifestyle, the one that had earned her such a bad reputation, hadn't been all that different from his own. He'd bounced from girl to girl, toying with each one until he got bored and then moving on with absolutely no regard for their feelings—and no intention *ever* of making a *commitment*. Being a guy, he'd gotten away with it. He hadn't been branded with a reputation as *easy* and *fast*; the double standard worked in his favor.

Talk about unfair, Bruce thought. *And I know why I was running around—how could I have forgotten?* He'd dated around because, after losing Regina, he was empty inside. He turned to other girls—lots of them—to try to fill that space, but it never worked. Until he met Pamela. And then, he'd felt it in his bones, in his heart. His playing around was over. She was the one.

Bruce wrinkled his brow. *Maybe it was the same for her. Maybe she knew about my past, but she accepted me anyway. Maybe she knew her dating around was over, too, because I could fill the empty place in her heart. Maybe . . .*

He shook his head and quickened his pace. "Maybe, maybe, maybe," he muttered out loud. "A million maybes aren't going to get you anywhere." The thing to do was to get on the stick and *talk* to Pamela. He didn't know, though. After all the negative stuff that had passed between them, could they ever find their way back to the feeling they had when they first met?

Bruce's thoughts were disrupted by a harsh male voice, just ahead of him around the corner of the school building.

". . . parked right over there," the voice said. "C'mon, let's take a ride."

Bruce walked forward slowly, his body tensing at the belligerent and threatening tone. *Sounds like trouble*, Bruce suspected.

"But I don't *want* to go with you," he heard a girl insist in a strained whisper. "Now, please just leave me alone."

The blood drained from Bruce's face and he froze in his tracks. He knew that voice; he'd been hearing it in his dreams. It was Pamela.

"You didn't used to play hard to get," the guy joked roughly. "Hey, it's OK with me if you want the Sweet Valley High boys to think you're a virgin, but I know different, so just get in the car."

"I said no!" Pamela cried.

The fear in her voice stung Bruce like a whip, galvanizing him into action. He sprang forward, rounding the corner at full speed. The guy was big and broad-shouldered, and Bruce recognized him as a Big Mesa football player. He was a good fifty pounds heavier than Bruce was, but Bruce didn't hesitate for an instant. "Get your hands off her!" he roared. Pulling back his arm, he aimed a rock-hard punch at the guy's jaw, knocking him flat.

Bruce didn't spare another glance for the guy, who pulled himself to his feet and stumbled off, groaning in pain. He had eyes only for Pamela, huddling with her back against the brick building, her arms folded tightly across her chest and her face streaked with tears.

Bruce gave her a shaky smile, his own eyes brimming. "Are you OK?" he asked anxiously.

Pamela nodded wordlessly, her tears streaming faster.

Bruce knew there was only one thing to do. He had to stop those tears. He was going to dry them all, one by one, and then he was going to make sure Pamela Robertson never had another reason to cry, ever again in her life.

Stepping toward her, Bruce wrapped his arms gently around the girl he loved. "I'm sorry, Pamela," he whispered into the tangle of her hair, holding her close as she cried, "I'm sorry. I'm so sorry."

Chapter 14

The wet, salty wind whipped a strand of hair across Jessica's face and she brushed it away, turning to look up at Todd. "It's cool tonight, isn't it?" she murmured, pressing close to his side.

"Umm." He tightened his arm around her shoulders, but the gesture was automatic; there was no warmth in it. *He'd rather be somewhere else,* Jessica knew, *with* someone *else. . . .*

She pushed the thought from her mind as they strolled down the moonlit beach. She held on to Todd, both arms locked around his waist, as if she were holding on to a life raft, the only thing keeping her afloat in a raging flood. If Todd didn't know enough to be happy with her, well, she'd just have to work that much harder to make him see that they were meant to be together.

Because if Todd left her . . . if Todd left her, Jessica knew her life would become like this Thursday night: cold and dark, with the sea pressing close, the waves threatening to crash over her head, to tear her to pieces. . . .

"I like being with you," Jessica said boldly, raising her voice to be heard over the wind. "It's that simple, Todd. You know, I never did understand what you saw in Elizabeth," she chattered on. "I mean, even before she started wrecking people's lives and killing people, she wasn't exactly a prize. Everyone always thought she was so sweet and good, but I knew her—I knew the *real* Elizabeth. And she's cold and selfish and conniving. She uses people to get what she wants and then twists it around to make it look like she was doing *them* a favor."

Todd shot a startled, troubled glance at her. "I can tell you don't believe me," Jessica observed. "You want to hold on to your happy memories. I just don't want you to be fooled, Todd. Don't imagine she's wasting any time moping around over *you*. You were just a status symbol to her, a prop. You made her look good—love didn't have anything to do with it."

Todd shook his head. "It wasn't like that," he

said, pulling back from her slightly.

Jessica didn't relinquish her hold on him. "OK, OK," she relented, with an attempt at a playful, flirtatious laugh. "Have it your way. Cling to your fantasy. I won't be jealous of the past, of a ghost. It's the present that I care about. And you're with *me* now, aren't you, Todd?"

He shrugged, his eyes on the dark, rolling sea.

"I knew it would end up this way," she continued, laughing again, this time almost hysterically. "Remember the night of the Jungle Prom, Todd?"

Jessica felt the muscles in Todd's arms tense. "Remember?" he hissed. "God, I wish I could forget."

"But why?" Jessica wondered, tipping her head to one side. "That was the night it really started for us— for you and me. Remember? You were named Prom King and I was chosen Queen." She gazed up at him, her eyes glittering obsessively. "It was like a sign that we were intended to be together, just like this."

Todd stared down at her, his eyes wide with shock.

"What?" Jessica demanded. "Why are you looking at me as if I've gone mad?"

"Because you have," Todd said hoarsely. "Don't you remember, Jessica? That was the start of the whole tragedy. That was the night Sam *died*. Don't *you* remember?"

Jessica shook her head. She didn't want to remember *those* things. Why did Todd keep bringing them up? "No," she whispered, standing on tiptoe so she could press her lips against his. "No."

Steven checked the numbers he'd written on a scrap of paper. "One-thirty-eight Idlewild Drive, Apartment C," he muttered nervously to himself. "This is it."

He'd gotten Billie's new address from the university operator the day before, but it had taken a full twenty-four hours to screw up his nerve to make it there. And now here he was: standing on the sidewalk in front of her door, a bouquet of her favorite flowers in his hand. It seemed like such a corny gesture—flowers and an apology— but Steven couldn't think of any other way to get his message across. A letter would have been too impersonal; even a phone call didn't seem adequate.

Plus, if I called her, she might just hang up on me, Steven thought. *Not that she doesn't have a similar option here. I already know she's a pretty good door slammer!*

But he had to risk it. Nothing ventured, nothing gained. And in this case, there was so *much* to be gained. . . .

Steven raked a hand through his dark hair and

took a deep breath. Then he knocked on the door.

His heart pounded out the seconds. One, two, three, four, five . . . *It's nine o'clock—maybe she's at the library, studying,* he guessed, after waiting for what seemed an interminable time. *Maybe she's out to dinner. On a date . . .*

He started to turn away, chastising himself for being so presumptuous, for imagining he was entitled to be a part of her life anymore. Then the door eased open, and Billie looked out at him, her eyes round with surprise.

She didn't slam the door in his face, as he was afraid she might. Steven's knees nearly buckled with relief and gratitude.

"Billie," he said softly. "I . . . I owe you an explanation. I owe you an apology." He held out the flowers. "These are for you."

Billie looked at the flowers, and then she looked back up at Steven. And then she smiled.

Instead of reaching for the flowers, she reached for his hand. Steven gave it to her, his soul flooding with joy, and for an endless, perfect moment they just stood in silence, smiling at each other and knowing that everything was going to be all right.

Elizabeth sat next to the swimming pool in the backyard, her arms clasped around her knees and her face tilted to the star-filled sky. The night breeze raised goose bumps on her skin, but she barely noticed the chill in the air. She was waiting for something, listening.

After a long while, she heard it: the sound of a car in the driveway. A door slammed, and then another. Then the engine revved again, the sound receding as the car drove away.

Elizabeth rose to her feet and walked back into the house to talk to Jessica.

Their parents were asleep; the house was dark, except for the kitchen. Elizabeth found Jessica standing at the counter, pouring herself a glass of orange juice. "Hi," Elizabeth said tentatively.

Jessica didn't answer; she didn't even glance in her sister's direction.

I have to keep trying, Elizabeth determined. *I have to keep trying to bridge this gap between us, or soon it will be so wide I'll never be able to reach across it.* It was one thing to lose Todd; that was terrible enough. But she couldn't live without her sister.

"Did you have a nice time tonight?" she asked.

Jessica turned slowly to look at Elizabeth. "Yes, I did," she replied, her voice as blank as her eyes. "I was with Todd."

Elizabeth gulped. Jessica smiled. "We *did* have a nice time. A *very* nice time," she emphasized.

"I . . . I'm glad," Elizabeth stuttered. "I . . . I

don't mind that you're dating him," she added, lying. "I only want for you and me to talk again, Jessica. I can't stand this."

The smile never left Jessica's face. Placing her glass carefully on the counter, she turned on her heel and walked from the room.

"Jessica, please," Elizabeth whispered after her.

The words fell into emptiness. Elizabeth stared into the dark hallway where her sister had disappeared. *What has happened to her?* Elizabeth wondered desperately. *What have I done to her?* Jessica wasn't just mourning Sam's death; she wasn't just sad. She was *different*. She was turning into a person Elizabeth feared she would never know, never be close to, again.

Margo stood in the middle of her room at a boardinghouse in downtown Sweet Valley and stretched her arms over her head with a luxurious yawn. She felt wonderfully refreshed: she'd showered, slept, and had something to eat. She was ready.

Sitting down at the small desk, she briefly scanned the want ads in the local paper. She'd assessed her financial situation, and even with the money from the pawned jewelry, she'd need to find a job fairly quickly if she didn't want to end up back on the street.

I'll read through those later, Margo decided, tossing the *Sweet Valley News* aside and reaching for the Los Angeles paper. First she wanted to see if there'd been any news about her. . . .

She flipped through the pages, skimming the headlines, a smile slowly spreading across her face. Still nothing, despite that hassle with Josh Smith at the L.A. train station!

Margo couldn't believe it. "Josh was lying," she cackled out loud. "The police were never after me. They don't know anything! I made it—I'm in the clear."

She was still chuckling when the name "Elizabeth Wakefield" jumped out at her.

Elizabeth Wakefield! Margo thought, gripping the paper tightly. *The girl in my picture!*

Quickly, she read the article, her eyes widening with astonishment. "She was on trial, but she was acquitted," Margo murmured. "'Charged with vehicular manslaughter . . . the night of the Sweet Valley High prom . . . confession by surprise witness . . . Elizabeth Wakefield found not guilty in the death of her twin sister's boyfriend, Sam Woodruff . . .'"

Twin sister? Margo froze, but inside, her brain was whirling and every nerve in her body tingled. She'd always wanted a *twin* sister.

Slowly, Margo reached for the shopping bag

that sat on the floor next to the bed and pulled out a blond wig. Walking over to the wall, she stood in front of the mirror. Carefully, she placed the wig on her head, tucking away every last wisp of dark hair, working methodically. When she was done, she stood for a long moment, drinking in the transformation. She'd changed the color of her hair . . . and changed her identity. Now all she needed were blue-green contact lenses.

Satisfied, Margo turned away from the mirror. Picking up her purse, she headed for the door. *Twin sister,* she thought, something clicking as the final puzzle piece fell into place and a plan gelled in her brain. *I am Elizabeth Wakefield, and I have a twin sister.* She smiled, the tiny dimple in her left cheek deepening. *Watch out, Sweet Valley!*

Get ready for Jessica and Elizabeth's hottest adventures ever when they go to **SWEET VALLEY UNIVERSITY**!

Join Lila, Todd, Enid, and all your favorite Sweet Valley characters as they become wilder and *wiser in* Love, Lies, and Jessica Wakefield *due in October!*

Here's an exciting excerpt from SVU #2,
Love, Lies, and Jessica Wakefield

It was an off-campus party, filled with loud music, laughter, and handsome guys, but still Celine Boudreaux was bored.

Idly playing with the miniature white rose she'd taken from the vase beside her, she stared back at the attractive but exhaustingly dull guy in front of her. His name was either Darren or Daryl and he was a philosophy major. For some reason he was trying to seduce her by explaining Aristotle's ethics to her. Celine wasn't interested in anybody's ethics. Ethics were like rules; they cramped your style.

"Excuse me," she said in her soft, sexy drawl. "But I just want to go refill my glass."

Even though he'd been in the middle of a sentence, he smiled back at her.

That was the advantage of having a Southern accent among Yankees. No matter what you said, they thought it must be something nice.

Without a backward glance, Celine floated out of the room, her perfume drifting behind her like a train of blossoms. She could feel the eyes on her. Celine considered her Granny to be a first-class witch in many ways, but she had to admit that her Granny often gave good advice. Always make an entrance and always make an exit, her Granny had always told her. And that's what Celine always did.

Coming into the kitchen, she caught her reflection in the window over the counter. *You look gorgeous,* she told herself, pouring another drink. *You look stunningly, devastatingly, eat-your-heart-out gorgeous.*

Behind her, in the window, she could see other reflections. There was a drippy guy from her English class, and Nina Something from her hall.

And suddenly there appeared someone she'd been looking for all night. The reflection showed a young man wearing an expensive black linen suit. He was as beautiful as a fairy-tale prince. And he looked as bored as she felt.

A shadow crossed Celine's heart. She was extremely good at manipulating people. There were very few people she couldn't get around. One was her ghastly roommate, Elizabeth Goody-Two-Shoes Wakefield. The other was standing behind her, talking to a guy who looked as if one of his parents must have been a tank.

Celine took a deep breath and swung slowly around. She was good at getting what she wanted. And she wanted the young man in black like she had never wanted anyone—if only because he didn't want her.

"William!" she gushed, gracefully sliding between him and the tank, and tapping the flower against his chest. "I didn't know you were here. What a nice surprise!"

He looked from her to the rose. For just a second the bored expression in his eyes was replaced with something else: disdain. Then he took the flower from her hand and went on talking as though she weren't there. He sounded just a little bit drunk.

"It sounds to me like your friend went to the wrong part of Mexico," he said to the guy. "It's too bad you didn't tell me he was going. I could have recommended an incredible beach."

Celine's smile grew brighter. "Oh, Mexico." She sighed. "I love Mexico. Isn't it just the most romantic place?"

William continued to ignore her, but the tank

began to speak. "Um . . . uh . . . William," he said, his eyes on Celine. "I don't believe I've met your friend."

William looked at him blankly. "My friend?"

It was times like these that Celine wished her Granny was a real witch. If she were, Celine would be able to put a spell on William White that would destroy his happiness for the rest of his life.

"Celine," she said, her voice as soft as velvet and as sweet as pecan pie. "Celine Boudreaux."

The tank grabbed her hand so roughly she thought he was going to shake it loose from her wrist. "I'm glad to meet you, Celine. I've wanted to since the beginning of year. I'm Steve Hawkins." He grinned at her mindlessly. "I've seen you around."

Well, I haven't seen you. She looked down for a second, so he would think she was blushing modestly. *And if I had, I would've run.*

"You mean you noticed me?" she whispered. "You noticed little old me in a school this big?"

Impossible though it seemed, the grin became even more mindless. "I'd notice you anywhere."

"Did you hear that, William? Your friend's been wanting to meet me." Celine glanced over her shoulder.

William White was gone.

Celine stared at the space where William had

been, her pretty mouth set in a smile as hard as industrial steel. The fact that she hadn't been able to turn William White into a horned toad or a hunchback with black teeth and b.o. wasn't really important. She was going to destroy his happiness anyway. Totally and completely. It was just going to take her a little longer to do without the help of witchcraft.

Elizabeth spent so much time in the library that by now she usually found a few familiar—even friendly—faces in the study carrels. Tom Watts, Elizabeth's boss at the TV station, was often there, working late. So was Nina Harper, who lived on her floor in Dickenson Hall, and who seemed to be one of the few girls on their hall who hadn't completely fallen under Celine's spell. And then there was the coolly handsome blond man with the glacier eyes, William White. At least two or three times a week Elizabeth found him sitting at the back when she arrived, watching her as though he'd been waiting just for her.

But none of them were in the library tonight. The only students bent over the desks were people who, like Elizabeth, obviously had nothing else to do. The losers of Sweet Valley U.

Stop feeling sorry for yourself, Elizabeth scolded, trying to concentrate on what H. F.

Mullerman had to say about the wit and irony of Jane Austen. But she couldn't stop feeling sorry for herself. Seeing Enid had upset her too much.

Elizabeth stared blankly at the page in front of her. It wasn't really Enid that had upset her. She was relieved that she and Enid were at least speaking again. It was because talking about the basketball team had made her start thinking about Todd again.

Sometimes Elizabeth almost thought that she was over the break-up. It had been her decision as much as his. Todd had wanted to take their relationship further than she was prepared to go. He seemed to think that now he was a Big Man on Campus Elizabeth should automatically want to sleep with him; but Elizabeth hadn't wanted to. She'd wanted to get used to her new world with all its new experiences and feelings before she made a commitment like that. A vision of Todd and her, holding each other as they had the night before school started, covered the page of Professor Mullerman's flawless prose. Elizabeth brushed away a tear. Sometimes she thought she was over him; other times she knew she wasn't.

Unable to concentrate, Elizabeth checked her watch. It was getting late, but not late enough to go back to the dorm. Elizabeth couldn't do that until she was sure she'd fall asleep right away. The last thing she wanted was to be awake when Celine got back. Celine sober in the middle of the day was bad enough, but Celine after she'd been partying all night was unbearable. They almost always wound up having a fight.

Elizabeth pushed her notebook aside with a sigh. Maybe she'd just lean back and close her eyes for a few minutes, try to re-energize herself. All she needed was to relax a little. From somewhere behind her, cellophane crackled.

Her eyes snapped open. *I don't believe this. Somebody's eating!* If it wasn't her broken heart giving her a hard time, it was her stomach.

This is really unfair, she said to herself. *You're not supposed to eat in the library. It's against the rules.* There was another crackle of a wrapper being torn, this one from the other side of the aisle. She was sure she could smell chocolate.

I can't take this. I'll have to go get a cup of coffee. Elizabeth started gathering her things together.

"I knew I'd find you here."

Every thought in Elizabeth's head drained away. She had never heard that voice before—not this close, not speaking to her—but she knew before she raised her eyes whose voice it was. She looked up to find herself staring into a pair of blue eyes so light they looked like ice.

He had a smile that was as secretive as it was dazzling. Elizabeth could never decide whether she thought the secrets it hid were good or bad.

He leaned against the carrel. His eyes might be cool, but his breath was warm. Warm and smelling faintly of wine.

"Tell me one thing," he whispered. "What's someone like you doing in the library on a night shot-through with stars?"

She said the first thing that came to her mind. The truth. "Jane Austen."

"Well, I certainly wouldn't want to deprive Jane Austen of your company." He lifted his hand. "But I got this for you."

Elizabeth took the delicate white flower and stared at it for several seconds, not quite knowing what to say. It didn't matter. When she looked up again, William White was gone.

☎
1 (800) I LUV BKS!

If you'd like to hear more about your
favorite young adult novels and writers . . .
OR
If you'd like to tell us what you thought
of this book or other books
you've recently read . . .

CALL US at 1(800) I LUV BKS
[1(800)458-8257]

You'll hear a new message about books and
other interesting subjects each month.

**The call is free to you, but please get
your parents' permission first.**

MURDER AND MYSTERY STRIKES

SWEET VALLEY HIGH

America's favorite teen series has a hot line of

Super Thrillers! ®

It's super excitement, super suspense, and super thrills as Jessica and Elizabeth Wakefield put on their detective caps in the SWEET VALLEY HIGH SUPER THRILLERS! Follow these two sleuths as they witness a murder...find themselves running from the mob...and uncover the dark secrets of a mysterious woman. SWEET VALLEY HIGH SUPER THRILLERS are guaranteed to keep you on the edge of your seat!

YOU'LL WANT TO READ THEM ALL!